Michael Innes is J. I. M. Stew... Edinburgh Academy and Oriel College, Oxford University, he has been Student of Christ Church, Oxford, since 1949 and Reader in English Literature at the University of Oxford since 1969. His publications include *Character and Motive in Shakespeare*, *Eight Modern Writers* (the final volume in the monumental *Oxford History of English Literature*), *Rudyard Kipling*, *Joseph Conrad*, *Thomas Hardy*, and a series of novels. Under the pseudonym of Michael Innes, Dr. Stewart is the author of a number of witty and erudite novels of suspense, including *An Awkward Lie*, *Candleshoe* (originally published as *Christmas at Candleshoe*), and *Hamlet, Revenge!*, published by Penguin Books.

ALSO BY MICHAEL INNES

THE AMPERSAND
PAPERS

MICHAEL INNES

PENGUIN BOOKS

Penguin Books Ltd, Harmondsworth,
Middlesex, England
Penguin Books, 625 Madison Avenue,
New York, New York 10022, U.S.A.
Penguin Books Australia Ltd, Ringwood,
Victoria, Australia
Penguin Books Canada Limited, 2801 John Street,
Markham, Ontario, Canada L3R 1B4
Penguin Books (N.Z.) Ltd, 182–190 Wairau Road,
Auckland 10, New Zealand

First published in Great Britain by
Victor Gollancz Ltd 1978
First published in the United States of America by
Dodd, Mead & Company 1979
Published in Penguin Books 1980

LIBRARY OF CONGRESS CATALOGING IN PUBLICATION DATA
Stewart, John Innes Mackintosh, 1906–
The Ampersand papers.
Reprint of the 1979 ed. published by Dodd,
Mead, New York, in series: A Red badge novel of
suspense.
I. Title.
[PZ3.S85166Aj   1980]   [PR6037.T466]   823'.912   80-17646
ISBN 0 14 00.5163 5

Printed in the United States of America by
Offset Paperback Mfrs., Inc., Dallas, Pennsylvania
Set in Baskerville

PART ONE

LITERARY RESEARCH AT
TRESKINNICK CASTLE

I

WHO KNOWS WHAT may be buried in his back garden? Only the man who has cultivated the whole area to a considerable depth. If his spade strikes on something out-of-the-way—the golden helmet, perhaps, of some Roman general, or an Anglo-Saxon *scramasax* exquisitely inlaid with copper, silver, niello and bronze—it is likely to be what the law describes as treasure trove. No owner can conceivably be discovered for it, but this by no means makes it the property of the finder. The finder, indeed, must hasten into the presence of the Coroner (popularly supposed to deal only in corpses) and produce his discovery. The Coroner will then sit on it. He will hold an inquest on the object, that is to say, and pronounce upon whether it be treasure trove or no. To hold on to one's find and say nothing is an indictable offence. Or it is so in England. In Scotland natural cupidity and possessiveness is more mildly regarded, although at the same time more portentously dealt with, since those charged with weighing the matter include the Procurator-fiscal and the Queen's and Lord Treasurer's Remembrancer. In both countries there is, of course, a spot of dead letter about all this. The affair ends up—it may be crudely put—by everybody getting his whack.

Precious things have often been buried or entombed in a big way, with results more or less strikingly apparent on the earth's surface. One thinks of the pyramids. Or of that oddly shaped hummock near Woodbridge in Suffolk which proved to follow the lines of a buried ship: a clinker-built ship very like another ship found at Nydam in South Jutland. One had to go back to the year 481, it turned out, before anything like the splendour of the Sutton Hoo treasure had been buried anywhere in Europe.

Lesser treasures have been found in odder places. Particularly 'literary' treasures. In 1930, for example, at Malahide Castle near Dublin, somebody unearthed in a cupboard a box supposed to contain croquet equipment: it proved to harbour, among other things, the manuscript of James Boswell's *Journal of a Tour to the Hebrides with Samuel Johnson, LL.D*. To one section of the learned world this discovery was quite as exciting as Sutton Hoo had been to another.

These historical or antiquarian remarks are perhaps a shade on the portentous side as a prelude to some account of the Ampersand affair. But there is a link at least with the recovery of the Boswell Papers in that a certain element of obscurantism—even philistinism—in the landed classes is common to both. So is a castle. Lord Ampersand lived in one. He lived in it in increasing discomfort, since he was increasingly hard-up.

The Digitts—for that was the family name—had been for many generations perfectly ordinary and unobtrusive English folk. They had owned, that is to say, fairly large estates in the West Country (and numerous mines and quarries as well); they ventured with some regularity into the Army and the Church; occasionally one would take a fancy for politics, and occupy one or another of the parliamentary seats within the family's control. Ministerial office tended to elude these, surely the most public-spirited, Digitts. One, however, had become Under-Secretary of State for the Colonies in a rather short-lived administration towards the close of the nineteenth century. There was a

8

tradition that another had declined the distinction of being appointed Postmaster-General by Mr Lloyd-George, but nobody had ever found means of either verifying or confuting this claim.

The Digitts, however, produced (like the Coleridges, and numerous other respectable families) an occasional black sheep. Some had even dabbled in poetry—Dick Digitt, for instance, who in the mid-eighteenth century had drawn through rhyme's vexation a good deal of well-bred minor impropriety in the manner of Matthew Prior. And from time to time other Digitts, although not themselves creative, had been inclined to take up with literary, and even positively artistic, people. Nobody much minded; the morals of these eccentrics had no doubt been impaired by keeping such company; but it wasn't like gaming in a big way, or wrecklessly debauching young women in good society, with all the awkwardness between family and family, interest and interest, which can result from that sort of thing. But this minor strain in the Digitts, although it did frequently bob up, is very little documented, or indeed so much as mentioned by way of digression in such biographies and obituary notices as better-conducted Digitts attained to every now and then. It might almost be said that the Digitts in general, although aware of these occasional aberrations in their midst, had never totted them up; if they had, they would have discovered that they had seldom been without at least one such odd bod for more than a generation at a time.

And then somebody produced a little book about them. Or not quite as bad as that. The book was called *Some By-ways of English Literature*, and just one of the by-ways was them. 'A Step towards Parnassus'—that was the title of the relevant essay—was about a succession of Digitts who had briefly skirmished with the Muses, mostly in Youth. It was all rather twaddling, and it wasn't well-informed, and sometimes it was flatly inaccurate. The few serious journals that noticed *Some By-ways* condemned it as amateurish and belletristic: a hang-over from an age before scholarship had begun, so to speak, to give English literature the works.

Nevertheless this harshly assessed volume (the labour of a clergyman's widow, fond of books) alerted more competent persons— university professors and the like—to something they ought to have spotted and got on to long before. At one period and another, straying Digitts had hobnobbed, if only casually, with half a dozen major English writers or artists, and with countless minor ones as well. Lord Ampersand began to receive letters from members of the investigating class—most of them with American addresses—the general tenor of which was that his family had lately been discovered to merit regard. So would he kindly answer this question and that—and could he undertake to be at home in his ancestral seat or stately residence throughout the month of August, during which the writer would be vacationing in England. The writer's university, partly as a result of the writer's tireless efforts that way, was seriously considering the establishing of an archive in which the cultural life and affiliations of the Digitts would figure with proper prominence. And a visit to Treskinnick Castle might further this proposal quite notably.

Lord Ampersand was totally without experience of this sort of thing; he was conscious only of monstrous and unaccountable impertinence on the part of these grossly presuming persons; it was to be a quite astonishingly long time before the crucial penny dropped. He invariably replied that the multiplicity of his engagements precluded his entering into correspondence with the writer, and that

10

he never spent the month of August other than in Scotland. (There was another family castle in Scotland, but even more than Treskinnick it was a mere rat-hole of a place, surrounded by moors as denuded of grouse as of Great Auks and Dodos.) Occasionally there were more awkward because more circumspect approaches from indigenous learned persons: fellows of Oxford (or at least Cambridge) colleges who opened fire with letters of introduction from men Lord Ampersand knew quite well. To these impeccably accredited pests Lord Ampersand caused Lady Ampersand to reply, saying something about her grave anxieties over her husband's health, and their hope that something might be contrived by way of meeting in a twelve-month's time.

Then people began actually to turn up on the door-step (or beneath the portcullis) of Treskinnick totally unheralded. Several even got into Lord Ampersand's presence, and had therefore to be treated with courtesy—or what Lord Ampersand considered to be that. It was altogether vexatious and insupportable. Lord Ampersand, after serious consultation with his son-and-heir Lord Skillet (Lord Ampersand was the sixth marquess), gave orders that his personal standard was no longer to be flown from the West Tower to apprize the world that he was in residence. But this measure proved to carry no great effectiveness, since only the nobility and gentry (and of course the local people generally) had the significance of such a flag at all securely lodged in their heads. However, the servants were instructed simply to tell any unfamiliar visitor that neither his lordship nor her ladyship was at home. This produced at least a breathing-space in which the beleaguered marquess could set his mind to work.

These people were all after what they called the family

papers, and it was true that there was a litter of such stuff all over the castle. The library, which its owner thought of merely as the place in which he occasionally consulted Burke's *Peerage* and similar essential works of reference, and to which he also repaired from time to time for a quiet read of *Country Life* or *Horse and Hound*, contained stacks of letters and bills and out-of-date inventories and rent rolls which had been thrust unregardingly into capacious chests and cupboards over a good many generations of Ampersand activity or its reverse. But that wasn't all. There were, indeed, few rooms in the castle that didn't harbour in desk or drawer or wardrobe minor accumulations of the same sort. So a radical clear-up would be the thing. Get whatever could conceivably be intruded upon by persons in the researching way bundled together and lodged in some forbidding and virtually inaccessible resting-place: a dungeon, perhaps, or something like that.

It seems probable that at this point Archie Digitt (Lord Skillet, in fact) again took a hand in considering the problem. There was undeniably something a shade freakish about Archie; it might even have been said that as an Ampersand he wasn't entirely sound. Archie had some very odd friends, and interested himself from time to time in wholly incomprehensible business enterprises. He also had a *penchant* for rather brutal practical jokes such as might have gone down very well among cronies during the reign of Edward VII, but which tended to render an archaic effect in the more anaemic age of the second Elizabeth. Archie cast his eye on the North Tower.

The North Tower of the castle was the one that pretty well jutted out over the sea a long way below. It had been so built, one imagined, in the joint interest of defence and sanitation. Behind the battlements crowning it there was a

lead roof in very tolerable order, but apart from the large
chamber thus protected it was substantially derelict. The
staircase—a spiral staircase in the upper ranges—had
largely crumbled into impassable rubble long ago. But this
didn't mean one couldn't reach the top storey, and indeed
the roof. Lord Ampersand's father had in his later years
developed an interest in birds, as it is perfectly proper for a
country gentlemen—or a great landed proprietor—to do.
The situation of Treskinnick Castle being as it was, sea-fowl
had become his more particular study, and it had occurred
to him that the top of the North Tower would be a peculiarly
advantageous perch from which to pursue this avocation.
But how to reach it? The fifth marquess was a man alike of
means and of resource. Carpenters were requisitioned from
here and there about the estate, and they constructed for his
lordship a wooden staircase, vaguely akin to those external
fire-escapes that run up the outer walls of multi-storey build-
ings, which began in the inner ward of the castle, presently
made a right-angled turn, and then rose to an aperture
admitting to the top floor of the tower. From this in turn a
trap-door gave access to the roof. The fifth marquess had an
excellent head for heights; as he went up and down his new
staircase it didn't at all trouble him that only a skimpy
hand-rail interposed between himself and vacancy; nor that
the whole structure, being somewhat amateurish in design,
wobbled a little when in use. His wife was terrified of the
whole affair, and wouldn't have dreamt of trusting herself to
it. But the fifth marquess saw a good deal of his marchioness,
one way and another, and enjoyed a certain sense of security
in his new aerie.

The sixth marquess took no interest in birds—unless,
indeed, he was squinting at them along the barrel of a gun.
He had never climbed to the top of the North Tower in his

life, and saw no reason to do so simply because he had become its proprietor. It therefore fell wholly out of use, and the wooden staircase became an ill-maintained, rickety, and treacherously slimy structure. The foot of it had even been encased in a tangle of barbed wire, since it would be annoying if some foolhardy visitor to Treskinnick tumbled off the thing and into the sea.

What Lord Skillet had thought of seemed itself attended with an element of risk. Why not constitute that large upper chamber something that could be called a muniment room; fix over the entrance to it, in a temporary way, one of those rope-and-pulley affairs used to hoist things up into warehouses; and then deposit in it by this method all the Ampersand papers that ever were? The sort of people who devoted themselves to antiquarian pursuits and crackpot researchings would certainly not be of a temper to remain undaunted by so arduous—indeed perilous—a path to knowledge. They'd take one look, and thereafter give Treskinnick a wide berth.

Lord Ampersand was at first rather shocked by the levity of his son's proposal. But as well as being funny, there was something faintly malign about it that appealed to the arrogant side of his nature; he indulged in a ludicrous fantasy of a wretched professor of something or other losing his nerve on that staircase, and being unable to budge whether up or down. Like the famous Duke of York, Lord Ampersand thought. He was recalling, with characteristic inaccuracy, an old song.

So this bizarre plan was actually put into effect. Everything that the Ampersands judged anybody might get nosy about (and the appearance, at least, was of there being several tons of it) was bundled into large skips and baskets, and then hoisted to its new home. Lord Ampersand, who didn't inherit his father's fondness for cliffs and chasms, directed operations from ground level. Lord Skillet ascended the staircase and surveyed results. Not being quite satisfied that an adequate effect of disarray had been achieved, he ordered the superimposition upon sundry stacks and crates of paper of a variety of objects not commonly to be found in repositories of the written word. An anchor and anchor-chain, a worm-eaten dinghy, and a decayed fishing-net together with some lobster pots witnessed to the marine situation of Treskinnick Castle; there were numerous stuffed animals—deer and badgers and foxes and otters and beavers—such as contemporary taste no longer judged agreeable in public rooms; and a good deal of furniture which had been more or less broken up by fractious children and disaffected servants during the preceding two or three centuries.

Lord Ampersand highly commended his son's diligence, and even entered so fully into the spirit of the occasion as to cause the printing of an engraved card, designed as being in future the sole reply that inquiring learned persons should receive. It read:

> Lord Ampersand takes pleasure in intimating that the Muniment Room at Treskinnick Castle will in future be open on the first Thursday of every month between the hours of two and five of the clock in the afternoon
>
> Railway station: Lesnewth: 15 miles
>
> Afternoon tea in the Old Stables: 60p

The Ampersand men were particularly tickled by the

final bit of information and its price-tag. But Lady Ampersand wisely censored it, pointing out that if several char-à-
bancs full of trippers were thus enticed to Treskinnick the
village women who would have to be hired to slop them out
their tea would demand an outrageous wage, so that the
venture must be a dead loss. Lord Skillet, who had long ago
ceased trying to make his mother see a joke, reluctantly
concurred in the deletion.

During the next few months perhaps as many as half a
dozen hardy explorers penetrated to Treskinnick Castle.
Of these the yet bolder ascended to the muniment room,
looked around them, and took their departure cautiously
but in evident haste. It became known that the present
Lord Ampersand was mad, that his heir was madder, and
that among their aberrations had to be numbered a wholly
perverted sense of humour. Quite soon the learned became
discouraged, and the family was left in peace.

II

'HERE IS A letter from Agatha,' Lady Ampersand said at breakfast one morning. (Agatha was Lady Ampersand's sister.) 'She encloses a cutting from *The Times*.'

'What should she do that for?' In Lord Ampersand's head it had been established long ago that Agatha was a damned interfering woman. '*The Times* comes into the house every day. I notice it regularly on the table in the hall. And Ludlow looks at it when he irons it, and tells me if anybody's dead.' Ludlow was the marquess's butler. 'As it happens, nobody has died for years, so your sister can't have sent you an obituary. So what is it? Not some rubbish about Archie being had up again for speeding, I hope.'

'Nothing of the kind. It's about somebody called Shelley. A poet.' Lady Ampersand gave thought to this. '*The* poet,' she emended concessively. 'He was in the books at school.'

'Shelley? I know all about him.' It pleased Lord Ampersand to show his wife from time to time that he was quite on the ball. 'Years ago, when I was at the House—'

'I thought you'd never been to the House, Rollo. Or not after taking your seat.'

'Not the House of Lords, my dear. The House. Christ Church.'

'Oh, I see. The Oxford one. Of course.' Lady Ampersand was a little at sea. 'And you met Shelley? How interesting!'

'Certainly not. Shelley was dead. He must have been,

since there was this memorial to him. That's what I'm telling you about.'

'Yes, Rollo. Do go on.'

'Once, when I was up at the House, I strayed into one of the colleges. I can't think why.'

'But isn't the House Christ Church? Isn't that just what you've said?'

'Of course it is. One ought to know these things, my dear.'

'And isn't Christ Church one of the colleges?'

'Certainly not. I was there for three years, and I don't recall such a suggestion ever being made. I strayed into one of the colleges, as I say, and there was this memorial to Shelley. Uncommonly indecent thing.'

'Would he have been one of the professors?'

'Something of the kind, no doubt. But what is this stuff in *The Times* about him?'

'It says he had a circle.'

'Shelley had a circle? Doesn't make sense. Might as well say that Shelley had a triangle. Or a trapezoid or a rhombus.' Lord Ampersand had brilliantly recovered these figures from studious Eton days.

'A set, Rollo. Shelley had a *set*. He came of very decent people in Sussex, it seems, although his father was only the second baronet. And some of his set were of really good family. Lord Byron was one of them. The sixth Lord Byron. He wrote even more poetry than Shelley did.'

'Long-haired crowd, eh?' It was plain that Lord Ampersand was not favourably impressed. 'You still haven't told me why Agatha has unloaded this rubbish on you. Ludlow, take away this toast. It's burnt.'

Ludlow, whose attendance at the breakfast-table was one of his employer's more outrageous insistences, judged that this injunction could be sufficiently obeyed by raising a single eyebrow to an assisting parlourmaid—who removed the offending toast so nervously that she contrived to scatter a good many crumbs down Lord Ampersand's neck. Lord Ampersand made no protest. He was always quite as well-disposed as was at all proper to the more personable of the female domestics about the place.

'Agatha's eye caught the name of Digitt, Rollo.' Lady Ampersand was now consulting the cutting received from her sister.'Adrian Digitt.'

'Never heard of him.'

'A son, it seems, of the second marquess's younger brother. There's quite a lot about him. It seems that he had a circle too. Or several circles. He revolved in several circles. Whereas Shelley revolved only in his own.'

'Balderdash, my dear. Utter balderdash, the whole thing.'

'No, I don't think so.' Lady Ampersand was a patient—sometimes even a persistent—woman. 'Agatha says it may be important. She believes that Adrian, although rather far out, may have spent part of his life at the castle. He had left his wife, you see. Perhaps because of all those circles.'

'Sounds a bit dubious, to my mind. But go on.' Lord Ampersand held his wife's wisdom in considerable regard, although he was not always entirely civil to her. She came of a large family and had been, he liked to say, 'the pick of the bunch'—whereas Agatha would have been the bottom of the barrel. 'Go on,' he repeated encouragingly. 'Did Adrian know this fellow Shelley?'

'Very well, it seems. The article says that Shelley was a difficult person, but that he was devoted to Adrian Digitt, and that it is now clear that Adrian was one of the two

19

people who knew how to manage him. The other was a man called Peacock—who was quite obscure, I imagine, and certainly didn't move in the best society as a Digitt would naturally have done.'

'Naturally not. But I still don't see what's important, or even quite proper, about a member of my family taking up with a lot of scribblers. And fiddlers and daubers too, likely enough. Except for Lord Byron, of course. He may have been all right.'

'It's really the review of a book, you see, that Agatha has sent. And she has marked what she thinks is the most important passage. It's where the writer says that few men in England can have been as widely and warmly esteemed by people destined to be famous as, it is now apparent, was Adrian Digitt.'

'That's very kind of you, my dear child. Put it down in front of her ladyship.' Lord Ampersand was speaking thus paternally to the parlourmaid, who had returned with a rack of more acceptable toast. 'But, Lucy,' he went on to his wife, 'does all this have any practical bearing on our affairs?'

The sixth Marquess of Ampersand has perhaps not figured so far in our narrative as a man of commanding intellect, or even of keen observation, extensive views, or wide reading. But it is undeniable that at this moment his mind was beginning to stir. If not stung by the splendour of a sudden thought, he had at least been pinched by the ghost of a perception.

'It *might* have a bearing, Rollo. Agatha points out that in the earlier nineteenth century—which is when all these people appear to have lived—they were excessively fond of letter-writing and diary-keeping, and that sort of thing. This Adrian Digitt may have kept a diary, and all sorts of people may regularly have corresponded with him. Lord Byron and young Mr Shelley may even have sent him poems, and things of that sort.' For a moment Lady Ampersand paused, as if thinking of embarking upon useful enumeration in the field of literature. But she thought better of it. 'There may be money in it,' she said.

'Money!' Lord Ampersand was really startled. 'How on earth can there be money in it?'

'Agatha says that, nowadays, things that people have just written can be almost as valuable as pictures they've painted.'

'We haven't many of *them* left,' Lord Ampersand said grimly. 'Even the decent family portraits gone under that confounded hammer.'

'Yes, Rollo, and it really is too bad. Let Ludlow give you more coffee.'

For some minutes the Ampersands continued their breakfast in silence—and with the dread spectre of aristocratic poverty making, as it were, a third at the board.

'Agatha,' Lady Ampersand presently continued, 'has asked somebody who really knows. It seems that a play of Shakespeare's—say the one about Hamlet—just written out by his own hand with a quill pen and so on, would probably fetch more money than you got for all those Romneys and Hoppners put together—or even for the Gainsborough.'

'Good God!' Lord Ampersand was now visibly agitated. 'All that stuff at the top of the North Tower, Lucy—do you think there might be a play of Shakespeare's among it?'

'I suppose there might be. But isn't an unknown poem by Mr Shelley more probable? Agatha has been working it all out, and she says that even that would be immensely valuable.'

'Impossible!' Lord Ampersand was really shocked. 'A

poem? It isn't decent. But good heavens!'—a fresh thought had come to him—'would you say that all those damned prying fellows that wanted to come around had wind of this sort of thing?'

'Yes—but of other possibilities besides this Adrian Digitt who had a circle. I've heard Skillet say that various Digitts have rather gone in for literature, and things of that sort, from time to time. I'm bound to say, Rollo, that nothing of the kind has ever been known in my own family.'

'No, of course not, my dear.' Lord Ampersand was thoroughly humbled. 'But—do you know?—if there might be money around in all that I'm surprised that Skillet hasn't been on to it. Always a smart lad, Archie, wouldn't you say? Nose for the main chance.'

'It just can't have occurred to him.' Lady Ampersand had her own ideas here, and they were not entirely to the credit of her son as a properly filial person. But upon this she judged it injudicious to embark. 'I think, dear, that it should just be looked into,' she said comfortably. 'Perhaps the vicar could help. Or Dr Morrison, who has that modest little collection of old china. Or it might even be possible to hire somebody to investigate. For we *have* got a muniment room, after all.'

'Hire somebody!' The boldness of this conception astonished Lord Ampersand. 'Young fellow from the varsity—that sort of thing? But would it be possible to get one with decent manners, eh? I could write to some fellow who runs one of those places, and ask him to turn up a stone or two and see what offered.' This image must have gratified Lord Ampersand, who chuckled softly. 'Yes, I could do something like that. Young fellow would get his keep, and a glimpse of how our sort live. Attractive proposition for the right man.'

'I think there would have to be a fee, dear.'

'A fee?' The noble Norman brow of Lord Ampersand clouded. 'Treat him to a spot of rough shooting, perhaps. Let him go out and fish. Mount him, if he can manage more than a donkey. Thoroughly generous arrangement.'

'Yes, Rollo dear. But I shall write and consult Agatha about it.' Lady Ampersand was quite firm. 'Agatha will know just the right people to ask.'

'As you please, my dear. Time I was walking the dogs, eh? Splendid morning.'

And Lord Ampersand, mildly excited by the astonishing ideas that had been put in his head, embarked on his day's common round.

III

Lord Skillet was the Ampersands' only son, and now middle-aged: although enterprising, he had never displayed any interest in matrimony. There were also two daughters, Lady Grace and Lady Geraldine Digitt.

Neither Grace nor Geraldine had been interested in matrimony either—or if they had, it had been unobtrusively and ineffectively, and they were now well past an age at which marriage is a sensible idea for a woman. When not engaged in charitable exercises either in London or abroad they continued to live with their parents at Treskinnick Castle. They mingled very little, however, in what their mother called the neighbourhood, meaning the dozen or so families of any consequence resident in the western extremity of the British Isles. They had been constrained as girls to attend numerous dances and similar social occasions; to plouter down chilly streams in pursuit of otters, and round and round prickly moors in pursuit of hares; to graduate from alarming ponies to horses more alarming still. But if physically timid they were strong-minded, and they possessed their own ideas about the responsibilities of their station. Now in their forties, they were held by their father in considerable awe. They kept things called Blue-books in their rooms. They ought really to have been MPs. But only Skillet was that—and for the frivolous reason that he was determined to have sat in both Houses of Parliament in his time.

Lord Ampersand's parents had provided him with only a

single sibling in the person of a younger brother, Lord Rupert Digitt, who had been killed when pursuing a fox shortly after marriage. (This had happened in Kent, an outlandish locality in which one simply *doesn't* hunt: but Lord Rupert had.) It thus came about that the heir-presumptive to the marquisate (and to the barony) was Rupert's son, a young man called Charles Digitt. Charles came around Treskinnick a good deal. He probably felt an eye should be kept on the place. It might eventually be saleable as a home for disturbed children, or something like that. Charles, because his fox-hunting father had married late, was younger than his cousins Archie, Grace and Geraldine. He was understood to be very clever, and to go in for advanced ideas. Archie, although he had declined the duty of siring an eighth marquess, rather resented the existence of this presumptive one. He had been known to describe Charles as a viewy brat. Lord Ampersand, while deferring to Charles's position in the family and professing to look forward to his visits, was inclined to get fussed when his nephew actually turned up. He felt it due to the young man to give him an account of the present condition of the estates and of the financial situation generally. But as he really knew very little, leaving all such matters to Skillet, he easily grew confused in his exposition, and felt that he was being suspected of concealing things. It amused Skillet to enhance this quite baseless impression by himself adopting a shifty and conspiratorial attitude when appealed to by his father for facts and figures. Lady Ampersand, who under-stood the play of family feelings very well (although totally incapable of discursive thought on the subject), knew that Charles was not deceived or perturbed by this behaviour on the part of his kinsmen. And this was true. Charles was sure he wasn't being cheated because he was aware that there was pretty well nothing left that he could be cheated of. His uncle and cousin were already down to those entailed and settled remnants of the family fortune of which it was only the income that could come to them. (There had been a row over the Hoppners and the Gainsborough. But it had been decently conducted by lawyers. Charles himself had, so to speak, kept out of the picture.)

Of this distinguished but not particularly ramifying family only one further member falls to be mentioned at present. Miss Deborah Digitt was a spinster of mature years, who lived in a small but genteel way in Budleigh Salterton. This quiet resort (very little intruded upon by those vulgar hordes that in England seek the sea in summer), although it may be described as located in the West of England, was at the same time at a comfortable remove from Treskinnick Castle: comfortable, that is to say, if one is estimating what in the way of occasional attention is due to an obscure and impoverished relation. Lord Ampersand was very clear that he acknowledged the relationship; he frequently referred to 'my kinswoman Deborah Digitt'; he sometimes even said 'my cousin Deborah Digitt'. But he was quite vague about how the poor lady came in—a fact that may be established simply by recalling that he had never heard of Adrian Digitt, the revolver in circles. For Miss Digitt was in fact Adrian's great-granddaughter, and Adrian's father (as Lady Ampersand had discovered) had been the second marquess's younger brother. So Lord Ampersand's and Miss Deborah's ancestor in common was the first marquess.

Lord Ampersand—in a manner perhaps uncharacteristic of his kind—simply didn't know about all this. But the old soul in Budleigh Salterton was a relation, and he regularly sent her a Christmas card, and also occasional presents of game. What Miss Digitt (who lived ministered to by a single maid, of years even more advanced than her own) can have done with two brace of pheasants or a haunch of venison was unknown. But she always acknowledged these gifts correctly and without effusion. So Lord Ampersand had a comfortable sense that he did the old girl quite well.

If anybody did know whose great-granddaughter Miss Digitt might be it was probably Lord Skillet—who owned, however, a trick of keeping things to himself. But it was known in the Ampersands' household that Archie, oddly enough, called in on the old lady from time to time on his way to or from London—divagating from the main Exeter road for the purpose. He couldn't have done this from a sense of duty, since demonstrably he hadn't been born that way. Deborah must have amused him. But it was difficult to see how. On one occasion Archie had taken his cousin Charles with him to Budleigh Salterton. It had been a mid-morning call, and their kinswoman had offered them a glass of madeira and a slice of cake. She seems not to have struck Charles as she regularly struck Archie. Charles said that she was a cultivated old creature with wide-ranging interests. Archie said that she was simple-minded, and that if she had her childhood over again now (and in a sense she was so having it) she would be classified by busybody psychologists as ESN. Lord Ampersand's curiosity was unstirred by these disparate estimates. He just continued to despatch to Budleigh Salterton (when there was a glut of them) his sundry trophies of the chase.

Lord Skillet, as became the dignity of his father's immediate heir, enjoyed an independent establishment in a respectable manor-house a few miles from the castle. But being a legislator (at present of the elected, but eventually to be of the hereditary sort), he had to spend a good deal of his time in London: in addition to which he had various commitments, responsibilities and attractions (some of them not to be too curiously inquired into by his parents) in other parts of the country, and indeed of the globe. Of late, however, he had been round and about the castle a good deal, and had been showing what Lord Ampersand judged to be a laudable interest in the day-to-day running of the estate. Lady Ampersand had seen to it that a bedroom, bathroom and sitting-room were in permanent readiness for him should he be minded to pernoctate at Treskinnick: this since she had remarked that Archie and his father were prone to end an evening in a somewhat convivial way. Archie was a very fast, almost a reckless driver of high-powered cars, and it was undesirable that he should be let loose even on unfrequented country roads at too late an hour.

This being the way the Digitts lived now, it wasn't long before Archie was apprized of his aunt Agatha's discovery about Adrian Digitt and his circles. If it wasn't news to him (and his mother suspected it was not), it was news to his sisters—who proved to be not favourably impressed by it when the matter was eventually debated at a family dinner-table. Lady Grace was two years younger than Lord Skillet, and a little prone to be at odds with him over anything that turned up. She had now served for some years on the County Council, and been active on sundry other public bodies as well; and what she judged to be her brother's ineffectiveness and indeed incompetence as an MP irritated her a good deal. Lady Geraldine, two years younger again, generally followed her sister's lead, but occasionally darted ahead of it. At the moment they were both taking the line that Adrian Digitt had probably been no credit to the family.

28

'But, Grace,' Lady Ampersand said pacifically, 'the young man—of course he was once a young man—certainly died more than a hundred years ago. Nobody minds having quite shocking ancestors as long ago as that. In fact, everybody has.'

'There is no reason to believe him to have been shocking, mama. But it does look as if he gave most of his time to cultivating friends and acquaintances who were perhaps all very well in their way. A literary and artistic way, and so forth. But for a Digitt it was most unsuitable. Geraldine, do you agree with me?'

'Yes, Grace, of course I do. It seems not even to have been just a hobby. Was this Adrian in the army? Apparently not. Then he ought to have become a clergyman. If he was all that brainy he might have been made a bishop. As it is, I don't think we ought to start a fuss about him.'

'My dear children,' Lord Skillet said lazily, 'you are both talking the most terrible nonsense. The point is that there might be money in the chap. Aunt Agatha is quite right there. Adrian may have been a mere dilettante himself, contributing not at all to the public life of the country, and all that. He may never have peered into a Blue-book, or made a spirited speech about agricultural wages and tied cottages.' Archie grinned wickedly at Grace. 'But if he tagged around with Shelley and heaven knows who then he may have left one thing and another that could be turned into hard cash tomorrow.'

'Tomorrow, Archie?' Lord Ampersand, who tended to turn somnolent towards the end of a meal, had sat up abruptly. 'Did you say tomorrow?'

'C'est une façon de parler, mon père.' Archie knew that incomprehensible scraps of foreign languages annoyed his father. 'But there's a big snag, you know—so big that I doubt whether we need bother our heads about Adrian Digitt. Suppose he received, and preserved, no end of letters and what have you from Shelley, Byron, Wordsworth, Peacock—the lot. There's not the slightest reason to suppose that the stuff is here at Treskinnick. Adrian was simply some younger son's younger son. He may never have been near this place except for an occasional week during his school holidays.'

'We seem to know nothing about him,' Geraldine said. 'So we may make one conjecture or another. Adrian may have judged it proper to deposit what he thought of as important papers with the head of the family.'

'To be put in the muniment room,' Lady Ampersand said. 'I suppose they had one then, just as we have one now.'

'We don't have anything of the kind.' Lord Skillet was suddenly impatient. 'Calling it that is a joke. It's just a big dump of useless family papers and general junk. Not that the prospect of its containing stuff of Adrian's is any the less likely because of that. But it's inherently unlikely.'

'We can't know till we look, Archie dear.' Lady Ampersand offered this wise remark as she prepared to lead her daughters back to the drawing-room. 'And you *have* been looking, haven't you? At least you've been up and down that dreadful staircase quite a lot.'

'I've rummaged, Mama.' Archie rose to open the door, but not before he had replenished his glass with port. 'I can't say I've come upon a new canto of *Childe Harold's Pilgrimage*.'

'No, dear—but of course you may.' Lady Ampersand was perhaps a little at sea over the meaning of this remark. 'And do go on talking to your father about it. It may be important. Your aunt thinks so.'

The ladies withdrew, and Archie brought up a chair beside Lord Ampersand. Ludlow, who had been privileged to listen in on the family confabulation so far, made certain ritual passes with decanters and the cigar-box, and withdrew. Father and son remained under the observation only of a few deceased Digitts—commemorated by artists too obscure to be of regard in the sale-rooms.

'Total nonsense,' Lord Skillet said. 'I suppose you realize that?'

'I'm not clear that I do. Of course I can't stand your confounded Aunt Agatha. Never could. Has her head screwed on the right way, all the same. Have to give her that.' Lord Ampersand was inclined to resent his son's assumption that his son's was the only brain within hailing distance of the Digitt family. 'And Geraldine had a point, you know which is rare enough with her, God knows About our knowing nothing about this Adrian chap. He may have lived here in the castle all his days. People do, don't they? Look at your sisters. Never out of the place for six months together. Hold meetings of Conservative washerwomen in the billiard-room.' Dimly aware that he was rambling, Lord Ampersand paused to collect himself. 'Adrian may even have brought Shelley and all that crowd to batten on the place. Rest-home for them when they grew tired of drinking champagne out of ballet-girls' dancing-slippers.'

'One certainly couldn't keep that up for long.' Archie, as he sometimes did, gazed at his father as if he were an exhibit in a zoo. 'But it's true we know nothing about this Adrian. I must have a go at finding out about him.'

'Much more important to have a go at those damned papers. At least they're now all in one place. And none of those Nosey-Parker fellows coming around any more.'

31

'That's certainly advantageous. But what you're suggesting, you know, would be an uncommonly time-consuming job.' Lord Skillet paused. 'Still, I suppose I could manage it.'

'Ah!' Lord Ampersand paused too. 'Would you know a letter of Shelley's if you saw it, my boy?'

'Yes, of course. I mean, I'd quickly learn to.'

'No doubt you have the head for it.' Lord Ampersand chose a cigar. 'But I think we ought to have a pro.'

'A pro?' The heir of Treskinnick stared at his father in astonishment. 'What do you mean, a pro?'

'Fellow who does that kind of thing at the varsity. Or in one of those museums or libraries. Plenty of 'em, I don't doubt. Your mother's idea, as a matter of fact.'

'I think it's quite unnecessary—a waste of money.' Lord Skillet paused to study his father—but not, this time, as if he were in a zoo. 'Still,' he said, 'it might be worth the gamble. If he turned up just one letter of Shelley's that another man might miss, he'd more than earn his keep for a couple of months.'

'Is that so?' Lord Ampersand was much impressed by this equation. 'Advertisement in *Country Life*, eh? Where they have the nannies and married couples and young gentlewomen who can drive cars and so on.'

'That would be just the thing.' Lord Skillet paused meditatively, and then at leisure produced an afterthought. 'Or look here — leave it to me for a bit. I'll inquire around — and no expense involved. I may draw a blank, of course. But I may find just the right book-worm type.'

'Capital plan!' Lord Ampersand was constitutionally averse to small cash disbursements. 'And no heel-taps, Archie. We'll go and tell your mother.'

IV

OUR SCENE SHIFTS to Budleigh Salterton, where Miss Deborah Digitt is giving young Charles Digitt tea. It may be recalled that Charles had formed a more favourable opinion of this mature lady's intellectuals than had his cousin Lord Skillet; nevertheless it was perhaps surprising that he had thus sought out her company again. Charles had a profession. Indeed, he had nothing but a profession, since his father, the late Lord Rupert Digitt, had very successfully cantered and galloped and jumped and raced his patrimony into the English grass and English mud well before his untimely death. Charles did have before him, of course, the prospect of becoming Marquess of Ampersand one day. But he distrusted it. He had no reason to suppose Lord Skillet either incapable of, or indisposed towards, woman. And he judged him to be just the type that marries shortly before scrambling into his death-bed, and there maliciously begets an heir when actually *in articulo mortis*. In addition to which, the business of becoming eighth marquess would probably prove to be nothing but a dead loss in the pecuniary way. So Charles had a profession. He was quite a busy young architect: too young, indeed, to be even up and coming, so far; but clearly of the kind that expeditiously achieves that reputation. It was to the credit of his family feeling, therefore, that he had thus found time to drink Mr Jackson's Earl Grey tea with his obscure kinswoman.

He was discovering—what he had perhaps glimpsed at

their first meeting—that Miss Digitt was the family historian. She could have given Lord Ampersand points at thumbing over Burke and Debrett. She had a family tree hanging, not modestly in a wash-place, but prominently in the hall of her unremarkable villa. Her cats, which occupied most of the chairs in her drawing-room, were clearly pedigree cats. Even her aged maid-of-all-work was distinguishably of the pedigreed sort, wielding broom or carrying coal-scuttle in what might be termed an armigerous way.

'Have you heard,' Charles asked his hostess, 'that there's quite a to-do at Treskinnick over family papers?'

'I hear very little from Treskinnick. It makes itself known to me chiefly as a smell.'

'A smell, cousin?' (Charles had decided that this somewhat archaic mode of address would gratify Miss Digitt. He had thoughts of presently abbreviating it to 'coz', which had a pleasant eighteenth-century ring.) 'I don't quite follow you.'

'Pheasants. They don't need to be hung. They *have* been—quite generously, and I presume by British Rail. Fortunately the cats are fond of pheasant. For venison they don't greatly care. But I have persuaded Jane to cultivate a taste for it.'

'I see. Well, the family papers don't smell—except, perhaps, of mystery or mystification. Or even obfuscation.' Charles had quickly discovered that Miss Digitt liked this sort of talk. 'There are plenty of honest-to-God papers, as you can imagine. But the papers that my uncle and aunt have taken it into their heads to be busy about might be called notional ones. Nobody has glimpsed them, so far.'

'It surprises me that they should care tuppence about them, whether notional or verifiably extant. Take a cress sandwich, Charles. I have been teaching Jane to grow cress on blotting-paper. My impression of the present Lord Ampersand is that he is well-meaning but scarcely well-informed. He is thereby the less embarrassing to his wife, no doubt. Knowledge of any sort would readily confuse Lady Ampersand.'

'It may well be so.' Charles found that he was enjoying Miss Digitt—the more so because she was by no means all of a piece. Hidden beneath this acrid manner was something positively skittish. Or perhaps it should be called romantic. She was capable of being quite excited by the attentions of a personable young man. He wondered whether in her youth she had proved a worthy Digitt in some amorous way. 'Yes,' he said, 'it is true that my Aunt Lucy is no blue-stocking. But the woman has a bottom of good sense to her.'

'I'm delighted to hear it.' Miss Digitt had greeted this further eighteenth-century touch with a malicious chuckle faintly reminiscent of Archie Digitt, Lord Skillet. 'But tell me more about those notional papers.' Miss Digitt was now curiously alert.

'They're supposed to be Adrian Digitt's papers. I expect you know about him.'

'I expect I conceivably do.' Miss Digitt's tone was suddenly freezing. It had been a bad slip-up to suggest that there could be doubt about the point. 'A future marquess,' Miss Digitt continued grimly, 'might well make himself aware of Adrian's place in the family—and even that he was my own great-grandfather.'

'Yes, of course. I apologize for being so stupid.'

'What you might excusably not know is that I am Adrian Digitt's only surviving descendant. Legitimate descendant, that is. By-blows there undoubtedly were.'

35

'That is most interesting.' Charles paused thoughtfully—much as if he meant what he said. 'Your great-
grandfather must have been a most attractive, as well as
most distinguished person. Everybody worth talking about
admired him. It's quite unaccountable that literary history
hasn't taken a harder look at him. As a link between two
generations, for one thing—rather like Landor, wouldn't
you say? But of course that's all Greek to the people at
Treskinnick. Except, perhaps, to Archie. One can never
quite tell about him.'

'I have heard ill of Skillet's morals.'

'Come, come, coz! We mustn't be censorious. Haven't
you got around in your time? It's unbelievable that you
haven't.'

This astonishingly bold speech went down well. The
spinster behind her tea equipage actually blushed. But she
came back at once to the matter in hand.

'If the Ampersands take no interest in literature and
the arts,' she asked, 'why should they concern themselves
over the possible survival of some of Adrian Digitt's
papers?'

'They reckon there might be money in them.'

'Money?' Miss Digitt repeated the word with *hauteur*.
'Dear me.'

'Yes—but quite a lot of money. And it may be perfectly
true. People are beginning to pay for important literary
manuscripts almost what they pay for scarce works of
art. And your great-grandfather hasn't been failing to
attract interest—and even bring enquirers poking around
Treskinnick. Scholars mostly, so far. But if anything
is really turned up there, the collectors will quickly
follow. Great institutions, too. American libraries, and so
forth.'

36

'My great-grandfather will be brought into the market-place?'

'Just that—and it's what has made the Ampersands do the very odd thing they've done. I haven't told you about it yet. Not all that time ago, they were considering the whole affair a nuisance, and they shoved every paper and document they could lay their hands on into as inaccessible a place as they could think up. But now somebody has put the money-notion into their heads, and they've decided to hire a professional archivist—if that's what he's to be called—to look into the entire mass of the stuff. I suppose he's going to be put up in the castle, God help him.'

'It is certainly odd.' Miss Digitt said this frowning; she hadn't quite liked to hear the hospitality of Treskinnick so brusquely aspersed. 'And just where has this large accumulation of material been concentrated?'

'At the top of the North Tower.'

'The North Tower!' Miss Digitt was almost unaccountably startled.

'Yes, it's pretty mad. Only reached up that crazy wooden staircase. But that was just the original idea, and by way of disheartening tiresome visitors. I suppose they'll bring it all down again now, and set this mole-like character to work on it in the library.'

'The plum-cake was baked by a reliable woman from whom I bought it at our church bazaar. Oblige me by trying it.' Miss Digitt paused until her visitor had done as he was told and commended her on the wisdom of her purchase. 'Charles,' she then said, 'you appear to me to be a reasonably sensible man. So be good enough to tell me whether you think this all nonsense.'

'It can't be done, cousin. I simply lack the information

37

upon which to base any useful conjecture. But perhaps you don't.'

'Would it be useful to know where my great-grandfather died?'

'Most decidedly it would.'

'He died at the castle, where he had been living in retirement during his last years. His uncle, the second marquess, was a kindly man, and much attached to Adrian. Unfortunately he too died at almost the same time, and there were immediate family disputes of one sort and another. The particulars have not come down to me. However, the main point is clear. Adrian closed his life peacefully at Treskinnick Castle, while still devoting himself to ordering his remains.'

'Ordering his remains! You mean arranging his funeral, and that sort of thing?'

'His literary remains, Charles. *Reliquiae*, I believe to be the Latin term. He had copious diaries to set in order, and a large correspondence with his friends. When he was very young he and William Wordsworth, who was his contemporary at St John's, used to exchange poetical compositions. With Coleridge, to whom Wordsworth introduced him, Adrian collaborated in an abortive tragedy. According to my grandfather, who was a person of cultivation, Adrian had simply thrust it away in a drawer, and it never again saw the light of day.'

'But that is perfectly astounding!' Charles came out with this while actually munching plum-cake, and found himself at the same time looking almost suspiciously at his hostess. Was it conceivable that the old girl was pulling his leg? The idea was a fantastic one. 'Have you ever,' he asked more calmly, 'thought of doing anything about the matter yourself?'

'I have certainly once or twice considered paying a visit to the Ampersands—they could hardly decline to receive me, were I to propose myself—and have some quiet conversation with Lord Ampersand about the possibility of finding the remains. But on the whole I have thought it best to wait on the event. And now, Charles, you tell me that the event has, in effect, arrived. With a professional researcher at work, anything of significance will be found—and will be published and edited and so forth by competent people. Money-interests may be involved, as you suggest. But with these we need not concern ourselves.'

'No,' Charles Digitt said. 'No—I suppose not.'

'I ought to tell you that I possess a very considerable collection of family papers myself. Perhaps I shall show it to you one day, and let you look over it. I have noticed a few pieces by my great-grandfather, which would appear to be of only minor interest. There may be others. I have not gone in detail into the bulk of the material, but my will directs that this should eventually be done. At least I haven't stuffed *my* papers away at the top of a ruined tower. Incidentally, were Lord Ampersand properly acquainted with the chronicles of our family, he would know that the North Tower has more than once before been made a repository of what may be called treasures. Including a beautiful maiden, Charles. A Baron Digitt is said to have incarcerated such a one there in the interest of most reprehensible designs upon her.'

'Do tell me,' Charles said—rashly, since he had no desire at all to hear this murky family legend. Now Miss Digitt made quite a thing of it—and lent it, moreover, a very rosy and sentimental colouring. In a way, Archie had been right about her; she *had* a simple-minded side, and it lay in the direction of romantic imaginings. A designing rascal—it occurred to Charles—would have little difficulty in turning her silly old head. The oddity of this being all mixed up with a decidedly astringent personality so interested Charles that he quite forgot to ask what other treasures the North Tower of Treskinnick Castle was reputed from time to time to have harboured.

V

CHARLES DIGITT FOUND himself giving considerable
thought to that small Budleigh Salterton occasion. It had
several aspects that left him guessing. Was it conceivable
that in Adrian Digitt there lurked a little gold mine?
Although almost forgotten about in the family now (except,
indeed, by his great-granddaughter), he had probably
been something of a legend in it once. And about legen-
dary relations the most exaggerated stories are likely to
start up, and to flourish for a time. The business, for example, of his associations with Wordsworth and Coleridge
—names even more tremendous than those of Shelley and
Byron—might well be an instance of this. Unknown poems
and an unknown unfinished tragedy! Charles, although he
had no particular interest in literary scholarship, knew that
such things would create a small sensation if discovered,
and that publishing them would be a profitable enterprise
for somebody. And he also knew, as he had hinted to Miss
Digitt, that there was a quite mad market for original
manuscripts of such a kind. Quite irrationally, such objects, if recently unearthed, would fetch far more money
than if they had been known for a long time. The fact was
an absurdity. But there would be nothing absurd about
profiting from the knowledge of it. Then again, what about
Adrian's own 'remains'? Suppose that, over a long period
of years, he had kept diaries as good as, or better than,
say Henry Crabb Robinson's? *Yesterday afternoon a long and
interesting conversation with William Blake.* That sort of thing.

41

The sky would be the limit. Or if not the sky, at least something well up in a financial stratosphere.

Vague thoughts of this sort had been with Charles ever since he had heard of the current goings-on at Treskinnick. But now there was something new and imponderable in the situation. Almost casually (or had it been that?) Deborah Digitt had intimated that she herself possessed a considerable body of family papers. Even if the treasure of Treskinnick proved to be a mare's nest it was conceivable that the treasure of Budleigh Salterton would richly reward some vigorous spade-work. And whereas numerous learned persons had received at least a whiff of what might be so bizarrely concealed in that absurd tower, and the Ampersands themselves might almost be described as in full cry after it, the possible secret of Budleigh Salterton appeared to be at present shared between himself and Miss Deborah Digitt alone. Or had Archie got wind of it? Miss Digitt had given no hint of this—and Lord Skillet, moreover, despite the occasional attentions he had paid her, seemed not to stand high in Miss Digitt's regard.

But Archie—Charles felt sure—was very capable of playing a deep game. He was quite clever in his not too pleasant way. Certainly he ought to be sounded—although with the greatest circumspection, no doubt. Even some sort of alliance with him was a possibility. Having arrived at this thought, Charles wasted no time. The eighth marquess-to-be rang up the seventh in his flat in town and suggested that it might be agreeable to have a meal together. Archie said it was a delightful idea. He didn't sound surprised. But perhaps he was.

The cousins met in what purported to be a Spanish restaurant near Trafalgar Square. It had been Archie's

choice, but this didn't appear to mean that Archie
proposed to play host. Indeed, he hastened even to
exclude the possibility that they might go Dutch. Like his
father (and a greater nobleman, a Duke of Argyle, as
described by Dr. Johnson) he was narrow in his quotidian
expenses.

'Nice of you to invite me,' he said easily, as he scanned a
dubious bill of fare. 'And I thought it would be an appropriate place.'

'Appropriate?' Charles was remembering how much he
disliked Archie. 'How so?'

'I'd avoid the *paella*, old boy. Oh! Because of all this at
Treskinnick. The treasure hunt.'

'Oh, that!' Not very successfully, Charles tried to
give the impression that Treskinnick and all its affairs had
been far from his mind. 'I still don't quite get your
point.'

'Doubloons and moidores and pieces of eight. Don't you
know that at one time the North Tower was supposed to be
stuffed with them? The old wrecked Spanish galleon story.
It attaches to any house of the slightest consequence on our
coast—just as do yarns of wreckers and smugglers. Highly
improbable that there's a word of truth in it. But not more
improbable than this Adrian Digitt vagary that the old
folks at home have started up with.'

'I've never heard of our Spanish galleon.' Charles said
this rather drily, since he had a strong suspicion that Archie
had just made it up—this by way of a devious approach to
something that in fact interested both of them much more
strongly. But then he remembered Miss Digitt's line of talk
about the North Tower and its former riches (which had
included a beautiful maiden) as a matter of family report.
So perhaps there really had been some sort of old wives' tale

about a foundered argosy. 'But I have heard just a word or two about this Adrian Digitt's lost papers,' Charles went on. 'You think it's all moonshine?'

'Oh, most absolutely. Have you looked at the wine list? The Rioja is probably all right, but I seem to remember they have a capital Haut Brion '66.'

Charles ordered Rioja. There were limits—particularly to go along with the food in prospect. And he wasn't doing any sort of sucking-up act on Archie. He was just proposing to himself a very cautious exploratory exercise.

'I don't myself see anything inherently improbable,' he said, 'in this Adrian's having dumped some papers in the castle. And I do vaguely gather he knew some quite interesting people.'

'It seems so. And I agree it's worth spending a few pennies—my father's pennies—on some sort of look-see. I'm arranging it, as a matter of fact.'

'I've heard that too, Archie. Bringing in a professional, I gather. Well, good luck to him. Have you actually found your man?'

'I rather think so. One has to be careful, of course. And there isn't all that hurry.'

'If the whole notion is moonshine, as you say, there clearly isn't any hurry at all—or only so much as will satisfy your parents that something is being done. By the way, have you had a hunt through the stuff yourself?'

'I've taken a quick look once or twice, Charles. But it's a grubby ploy: dust and mildew and cobweb.'

'So I'd suppose. And you didn't come on the slightest trace of anything interesting—either by or about this Adrian Digitt?'

'Nothing at all.'

'Suppose there *is* nothing at all up there in the tower. Would you say, Archie, that that's an end of the matter?'

'Obviously.'

'I don't think you understand me. The man must often enough have put pen to paper. And received letters and so forth from this chap and that. Isn't it probable that some portions, at least, of all this do survive—if not at Treskinnick, then somewhere else? Although I confess I've myself nowhere to suggest. If we knew just a few facts about his life, it might help.'

'Oh, I see.' Lord Skillet cast a speculative eye on his cousin. 'Perhaps this old mole we're hiring may run up a bit of a biography. It would be the orderly thing.'

There was a pause while a waiter poured the unassuming Spanish wine. Archie, Charles reflected, wasn't going to be easy to draw. But it seemed reasonable to believe that he knew nothing of Miss Deborah Digitt's papers. Perhaps it hadn't even occurred to him that she was Adrian's direct descendant. Of course he was bound to catch up on all this sooner or later. But at the moment it looked as if Charles had a good start in that quarter.

'Shelley seems to be the fellow that the learned chiefly associate with Adrian at present. But Adrian would have been older than Shelley, wouldn't he?'

'Definitely.' Archie had the air of a man who, although not yet admitting boredom, soon will be. 'So what?'

'I just wonder what his relations, if any, were with the first generation of the Romantics. Wordsworth and Coleridge, for example.'

'Search me.'

'Is there anybody who might definitely know?'

'There may be, or there may not. I'm not an authority on this business, my dear Charles. So don't treat me as one.'

'Who would the stuff belong to?'

'The stuff?'

'Archie, don't be tiresome. Those conceivably valuable papers if they conceivably exist.'

'I expect my father would regard them as his—particularly if it was at Treskinnick that they turned up. As being head of the family, and all that.'

'Suppose, Archie, that they constituted a substantial property. Mightn't the lawyers take a different view? Mightn't you have a case for having them regarded as heirlooms, so that you would yourself have a life-interest in what they produced?'

'As you might after me, Charles? It's a delightful idea. And what a helpful fellow you are! But I don't believe it for a moment. They're not the Ampersand Diamonds—not that there *are* any Ampersand Diamonds, worse luck. The heirloom business is all a matter of deeds and inventories and so on. You know that perfectly well. Let's be frank about this. My father would sell anything worth selling, and pocket the money. Or buy a pedigree herd with it, or what have you. There's no sense in the old boy—none at all.'

'Well now, let me make one more point. Have you thought about the law of copyright?'

'Copyright? My dear Charles, nothing of the sort could have the slightest relevance. We're talking of stuff that belongs with Noah's Ark.'

'You may be right.' Charles said this on a slightly dismissive note, as if their topic were pretty well exhausted and they'd better talk about something else. But he was wondering whether here was the deep Archie again. Was it conceivable that a clever man should be so ignorant as to believe what he had just said? Even if he was, it would again be a matter on which he would eventually catch up. But if this was it, Charles once more had at least a start on him.

Charles now talked about motor cars, a subject upon which his cousin was knowledgeable and quite pleased to converse. It was only at the end of the meal that they returned for a few minutes to the topic of Adrian Digitt. And it had once more to be on Charles's initiative.

'Have you got the length of short-listing your moles?' he asked. 'And might I be a candidate myself? Shall I run over my qualifications?'

'You must be joking.' Archie seemed genuinely amused. 'It has to be a pro. I thought you'd gathered that. It's what is firmly in my father's head. And, as I've already told you, I have one runner fairly well out in front already.'

'What's his name?'

There was nothing particularly impertinent about this question—or not as between cousins. But Charles had brought it out in a sharply interrogative manner which appeared to offend Archie, or at least to disconcert him. He had raised his eyebrows.

'Sutch,' he said coldly.

'Such as what?'

'Sutch is his name. His name is Sutch. No doubt it can be made fun of. He's Dr Ambrose Sutch. A very senior man.'

'How did you get hold of him?'

'Oh, just by inquiring here and there. Asking one person and another. Why do you ask? You seem devilishly curious.'

'You said yourself that one has to be careful. And it's a

position of trust, in a way. Sutch might prove to be Snatch, and start pocketing things.'

'What a suspicious fellow you are, Charles! But, of course, what you say is perfectly true.' Lord Skillet hesitated. He might have been a man weighing the wisdom of making a confidence to a not wholly reliable person. 'As a matter of fact, Charles, I have a slight suspicion that something of the sort may have been happening somewhere already.'

'I don't understand that, at all. If you don't believe there are any papers in the castle. . .'

'I said *somewhere*. And I didn't, you'll recall, turn down flat your notion that some of Adrian's effusions may lurk in some quite different locality. And the admirable Dr Sutch, being anxious to nail the job, has done a little preliminary research already. Apparently the first thing one does is to rake through the likely learned journals for any recent mention of the chap you're interested in. And there has been some interest in Adrian Digitt, as you know, on the part of the kind of people who write in such things. Sutch has turned up an affair of the sort in an American journal. By a Shelley fan, I gather. He reports that something or other of Adrian's has lately been acquired by a private collector in California, who is refusing even well-accredited scholars access to it. That's not uncommon over there, it seems. No striking commercial motive involved. Just dotty acquisitiveness. Sort of squirrel instinct. But it *might* be because this collector has come by what he *has* come by in some underhand way. That's not uncommon either.'

'It sounds plausible.'

'Of course it does. One of Sutch's jobs would have to be keeping a look-out for any further quiet goings-on of the same flavour.'

48

'I see.' Charles looked hard at his cousin, who at the moment was innocently pushing over to his side of the table the bill presented by the waiter. 'You mean that something like theft may be going on, we don't know where? That there really is a cache of Adrian's scribblings in existence, and that it is being unobtrusively pilfered from, and the booty being equally unobtrusively fed into the market?'

'You express the possibility admirably, my dear Charles, which is just what I'd expect of you. You haven't any ideas yourself as to where it might be happening, and by whose agency?'

'Of course I haven't, Archie. I've been taking no active interest in all this, at all. It has simply turned up in our chat during this very pleasant meal.'

And Charles Digitt produced his wallet, and extracted from it a couple of five-pound notes. He had a strong feeling that the little party had now better break up—break up and be thought about. Unsurprisingly, he was conscious that here might be deep waters. Did Archie really know about the situation at Budleigh Salterton? Was he actually suspecting his cousin of having already slipped into a pilfering role there? Was he in effect saying, 'Charles, my boy, have a care! Sutch is keeping an eye on you'? Or was the boot, so to speak, on the other foot? Perhaps Archie himself was the pilferer, and the field of his operations nothing other than the North Tower of Treskinnick Castle. This sudden communicativeness on Archie's part might be a ruse designed to deflect suspicion from himself if it did become known that Adrian Digitt's remains were beginning unaccountably to surface here and there. Was there anything impossible about this? Charles Digitt took another hard look at his cousin (and at everything he either knew or imagined of his cousin's character) and decided that definitely there was not.

With expressions of mutual esteem (and clearly in an atmosphere of deep mutual distrust) the two gentlemen—or the two prospectively successive noblemen—parted outside the restaurant.

VI

LORD AMPERSAND KNEW almost at once that he wasn't
going to care greatly for Dr Sutch. Dr Sutch was an egg-
head in the literal acceptation of the image; he was bald,
and had a massive domed forehead reminiscent of the
disagreeable people who know all the answers in competi-
tions in the field of Universal Knowledge mounted by the
BBC. Whether Dr Sutch in fact possessed Universal Knowledge was never to appear, since he turned out to be a man
wholly commanded by one thing at a time. At the moment
that one thing was the Ampersands. He always said 'the
Ampersands' when meaning all the Digitts who were
around or ever had been around. This in itself a little
irritated Lord Ampersand, who wouldn't himself have said
'the Marlboroughs' or 'the Salisburys' when he meant a
whole gaggle of Churchills or Cecils. Perhaps it wasn't
positively incorrect, but it was faintly wrong—which was
something a good deal worse in Lord Ampersand's view of
the matter.

Dr Sutch, moreover, was a pedant, by which is meant one
given to unseasonable displays of erudition. Having at least
a rapidly assimilative mind, he had got up his client's
family rapidly and in overpowering detail, and he lectured
the Ampersands on every aspect of it. Lady Ampersand
rather liked this. She had always felt it would be nice to
know a little about her husband's people, but the topic
was one upon which her husband could inform her only
in a muddled way. History was mysterious to Lord

51

Ampersand, even although he was constantly looking up such contemporary manifestations of it as were to be found in *Who's Who*. Dr Sutch, although not exactly a courteous man, had notions about courtesy, and one of them constrained him to feign the belief that he was never doing other than remind Lord Ampersand of circumstances and connections already stored in Lord Ampersand's capacious mind. Lord Ampersand was infuriated by this.

So the question quickly arose as to what was to be *done* about Dr Sutch. To have him resident in the castle presented formidable difficulties in the way of protocol. To receive him at the family table for long would be totally insupportable. He couldn't very well be told to go and mess with Ludlow. To have meals served to him in a private room (as had obtained under former Ampersands for attorneys, the visiting dentist, and people of that sort) would be cumbersome—and also, in some perplexing way, counter to the spirit of the time. So Lord Ampersand decided—reluctantly, since considerable expense would be involved—to have the fellow put up at the Ampersand Arms. It was said to be quite a decent little pub, and was no more than a couple of miles away. Dr Sutch tended to corpulence, so the walk would do him good.

The next question to arise was where this tediously learned person should prosecute his researches. Lord Skillet, when consulted, at first professed to favour the billiard room, but this was perhaps only to annoy his sisters, since it was to the billiard room that they regularly summoned the humbler females of the region to receive instruction on various aspects of domestic economy and godly living. Lord Ampersand himself vetoed the library, pointing out that it was his habit to do a great deal of reading there. He was inclined to favour bringing all the stuff down from the

North Tower to the old stables—where his wife had vetoed that promising notion of tea at 60p a head. Finally it was decided that the walk to and from the Ampersand Arms was not in itself adequate to the safeguarding of Dr Sutch's health. He had better tackle that staircase as well, and do his rummaging where all the junk was stored already. Lord Skillet discussed this proposal with Dr Sutch. Rather surprisingly, Dr Sutch proved entirely amenable to it.

Once established, Dr Sutch sprang another surprise, conceivably occasioned by a rapidly formed conviction that the comforts of the Ampersand Arms were not such as to commend a long uninterrupted stay there. His work at the castle, he explained, would have to be on a part-time basis. He'd put in Mondays and Tuesdays on what he called the Ampersand Papers. During the rest of the week he would be continuing his antiquarian research for the Duchy. Lord Ampersand was a good deal impressed by this, and agreed to it at once. It was quite something to be employing a fellow who was at the same time in the service—as it must be—of none other than the Prince of Wales.

Nevertheless, this looked like slowing things down. But now Lord Skillet made an obliging suggestion. Although he had found Dr Sutch for the job, it was only because his interfering Aunt Agatha had prompted his parents to insist on employing a person of that kind, and most of Archie's references to the 'pro' were of a satiric or derogatory cast. With unusual good-humour, however, he undertook to do some of the donkey-work himself. Sutch had pointed out that it wasn't only worm-eaten dinghies and triumphs of Victorian taxidermy that were plainly irrelevant to his task; there was also a great deal of mouldering paper which nobody could mistake for anything not fitly to be made a

53

bonfire of or chucked into the sea; if Lord Skillet had a go at that it would be a very obliging thing.

So Archie, too, turned up twice a week at the castle and pottered around the North Tower. It couldn't be said that he was in any direct sense keeping an eye on Dr Sutch, since on those days Dr Sutch was absent on his royal occasions. But he may have been keeping an eye on what Dr Sutch had been about.

And then Charles Digitt began to turn up occasionally as well. Was he, in turn, keeping an eye on Archie? This came into nobody's head. And as he turned up only at week-ends, when his cousin invariably had mysterious engagements elsewhere, he had the run of the place to himself. Lord Ampersand, as usual, welcomed the heir presumptive amiably enough; he explained to his wife, as he regularly and most conscientiously did, that Charles was entitled to know about anything that was going on at Treskinnick. And Lady Ampersand was delighted to have her nephew as a week-end guest. It was, she said, nice for the girls. This expression cloaked her persuasion that Charles had more than a cousin's fondness for Geraldine, and that some eleventh-hour happiness would be achieved by her younger daughter as a result. A marriage between first cousins, she knew, was sometimes disapproved of on mysterious eugenic grounds. But the vicar (and the bishop) would have nothing against it, and on other accounts it would be an extremely suitable thing. Lady Ampersand sometimes started to count out on her fingers the somewhat disabling span of years sundering her posited lovers. But she always wisely gave up when she had arrived at the number ten.

But at Treskinnick Castle for a time, at least in a metaphorical sense, all went merry as a marriage bell (as the sixth Lord Byron had remarked of the Duchess of

Richmond's ball before the Battle of Waterloo). It was true
that Dr Sutch, so far, had nothing to report. He appeared to
have a conviction, irksome but to his credit as a serious
scholar, that his commission was to delve into the entire,
and for the most part entirely unremarkable, chronicles of
the Digitt family. On one occasion he even announced with
satisfaction that he had 'got as far as the Civil War'. Lord
Ampersand, although not very well-informed on the doings
of Oliver Cromwell and Charles, King and Martyr, obscurely surmised that such massive public disorder could
only have occurred a long time ago—even longer ago than
Shelley and Lord Byron had occurred. But he was gratified
to learn (or rather to be reminded) that Treskinnick Castle
had been besieged and reduced in the course of whatever
had then been happening. It appeared that this fate had
befallen a great many other castles at the time, and it would
be rather humiliating had Treskinnick been left out. Lord
Skillet made fun of the irrelevance of this august historic
occasion to the present circumstances of the Digitts, which
were as reduced as the castle had been in the mid-
seventeenth century. But in this judgement Lord Skillet, as
it happened, was to be proved wrong.

A day came upon which Charles Digitt and Dr Ambrose
Sutch did meet. Charles stretched one of his week-ends into
a long week-end, and on the Monday morning made his
way up to the muniment room. It struck him as he began
the hazardous climb that he was at a slight disadvantage in
this proposed interview. He had a strong curiosity about Dr
Sutch, but there was no reason to suppose that Dr Sutch
had the slightest curiosity about him. No doubt the learned
man would be civil. Yet he might perfectly well feel that
here was merely a troublesome interruption of his dedi-
cated task at Treskinnick.

The North Tower being a very massive affair, the chamber immediately under its roof was as large as a modest banqueting hall. Abundant as were the accumulated treasures of the Digitts in a paper and ink way (whether in bound volumes and letter-books or in dispersed bundles either trussed up in string or merely flapping around) there was tolerable space to move about in. The deer, foxes, badgers and otters—and also numerous plaster-and-paint versions of improbable-looking fish—had all been moved to one half of the room, and had an odd appearance of patiently awaiting attention they weren't going to get. At the other end the various bits and pieces of nautical equipment had been piled up, one thing on top of another, in a higgledy-piggledy fashion.

Quite a lot of muscular effort must have been involved, and Charles wondered who had provided it. He couldn't imagine Archie doing much in that line, or Ludlow being at all readily persuaded to muck in. A species of *corvée* levied around the estate was no doubt the answer. Certainly in one way or another the decks had been cleared for Dr Sutch. Down the length of the room two long trestle tables had been set up, and on these were piles of paper presumably in process of being set in order. There were also a couple of large steel filing-cabinets which must have been hoisted to their present elevation at considerable risk to life and limb.

All in all, Dr Sutch's present surroundings didn't much suggest the dignity of scholarship; nevertheless Dr Sutch received his visitor with all the *aplomb* of the Director of the British Museum or Bodley's Librarian in the University of Oxford proposing to do the honours of his institution to one of the Crowned Heads of Europe.

'Mr Charles Digitt?' Dr Sutch asked with a grave bow.

56

'Yes, I'm Charles Digitt. How do you do?'

'How do you do?' Dr Sutch shook hands. 'May I venture to wish you many happy returns of the day?'

'Oh, thank you very much.' Charles had quite forgotten that it was his birthday, and it had been an occasion of which his kinsfolk at Treskinnick must have been culpably incognizant. 'You must be quite a chronologist,' he added rather feebly.

'A facility in committing dates to memory is a useful, if humble, endowment to one in my walk of life, Mr Digitt. It enables me, for instance, to remind you that the anniversary of your father's death falls the day after tomorrow. Lord Rupert would then be fifty-seven, had he been spared to us. A life most unhappily cut short in its prime.'

'Yes, quite.' Charles didn't altogether like this facile command of the family annals, although these particular instances of it were harmless enough. 'How is the hunt for Adrian getting on, Dr Sutch?'

'We cannot, things being as they are'—and Dr Sutch gestured comprehensively round the muniment room—'expect any very immediate success. But meanwhile, I am getting my bearings in a general way. It is curious to reflect that on his death-bed Adrian Digitt, as a devout Anglican, may have been distressed by the news of Dr Pusey's condemnation and suspension at Oxford following upon his sermon on the Holy Eucharist. That was preached, you will recall, on the 14th of May. It was an interesting year, seeing both the publication of Liddell and Scott's *Greek-English Lexicon* and the foundation of *The Economist* by James Wilson. Yet who is to say what was that year's most important event? It saw, too, the beginning of Sir Richard Owen's *Comparative Anatomy and Physiology of Invertebrate Animals*.'

'By Jove! Did it really?'

'Which was concluded in 1846, and enlarged in 1855.'

'Well, well!' Charles wondered whether he was being made fun of. 'Have you met Miss Deborah Digitt?' he asked abruptly.

'I have not had that pleasure.' Dr Sutch appeared a little startled. 'Do you recommend it?'

'It's just that she's a bit of a historian herself.' Charles at once regretted having mentioned this Budleigh Salterton connection. It was in his interest to keep Deborah out of the picture for the present. 'Knows a little about the family, and that sort of thing. But probably less than you do.'

'I must make a note of it. I gain the impression, Mr Digitt, that your father also took an interest in the subject. How unfortunate that he died before you were of an age much to discuss it with him.'

'I was two.' Charles felt some satisfaction in thus showing command of at least one chronological fact.

'But precocious, no doubt.' Dr Sutch seemed to judge that this inane remark was deftly complimentary. 'I have been working, as I have explained to my clients, on the period of the Civil War. Do the fortunes of your family at that period hold any special interest for you?'

'I can't say that they do.' Charles was conscious that Dr Sutch had put his question with an odd sharpness. 'I gather the castle got bashed about a good deal. It's a period that has its interest in the history of warfare, I suppose. Owners of places like this imagining they were still in the Middle Ages, and able to dig in and resist a siege. Then up come chaps with really powerful up-to-date cannon and start pulverizing them. This tower clearly suffered a bit. But it puzzles me, rather. I'm not a soldier, of course. I'm an architect.'

'Ah, yes. I don't doubt, Mr Digitt, that you will contribute notably to our national heritage in that field.'

'Thank you very much.' Charles judged this decidedly overpowering. 'I hope that crazy staircase doesn't worry you. The idea of it was to contribute notably to bird-watching, I believe. Its present use has been a whim of my uncle's, and of my cousin Archie's. I gather Archie has been lending you a hand.'

'Yes, indeed. Lord Skillet is being most helpful.'

'He seems a little worried by your discovery that some papers of Adrian's are thought to have arrived in a private collection in America.'

'He is rightly worried, of course. Yet I judge that anything of the sort is likely to be of minor importance.'

'I had a chat with my cousin a little time ago, as a matter of fact, about places other than Treskinnick in which some sizable cache of the stuff might be found. Do you yourself think there may be anything in that?'

'It is not a possibility to be neglected, Mr Digitt. As you know, there was the period of residence in Italy.'

'I don't know anything about a period of residence in Italy.' Charles felt something like his uncle's irritation at thus being politely credited with information there wasn't the slightest reason to suppose he had. 'Do you mean that Adrian Digitt lived in Italy for a time?'

'Most assuredly he did. For a substantial period before his final domestication here at Treskinnick he occupied the *primo piano nobile* of a small *palazzo* on the Grand Canal at Venice.'

'The dickens he did! That must have cost him a pretty penny.'

'Not perhaps at that period. But the fact opens up—does it not?—a further field of investigation. There may be papers mouldering away in Venice now.'

59

'But the story is, Dr Sutch, that Adrian put in his last years here at the castle in trying to set all his stuff in order. So he's not likely to have left much in Venice—or anywhere else on the Continent.'

With this argument Dr Sutch was constrained to agree—although obviously with reluctance. Charles felt it unnecessary to hint to him that Lord Ampersand was most unlikely to stand him the cost of a little tour in Italy on the strength of this nebulous hypothesis. Charles was coming to suspect Dr Sutch of being a humbug. He didn't know what kind of humbug, but of the general idea he was pretty confident. How had Archie come by the chap? It was a point on which Archie had remained suspiciously vague. Was Sutch what might be called a creature of Archie's? Or was he fooling Archie, or at least planning to do so?

These dark thoughts came to Charles partly because he sensed that Dr Sutch, for all his grave and deferential manner, was having dark thoughts about *him*. He had made no move to show Charles how he was actually going to work in the muniment room. It had been an unsatisfactory interview, and Charles resolved to put an end to it.

He moved to the door giving on to the little wooden platform in which the external staircase terminated. Although he had no particular fear of heights, he realized that he would be taking a firm grip of himself as he emerged and began the descent to the castle's inner ward. Only the sea lay at a crazy depth below. Or at least one could see only the sea; actually there was a narrow band of tumbled rock rounding the promontory on which Treskinnick lay, and along this one could make one's way at low tide. But to glimpse this from above one would have to lean out over the staircase's hand-rail in a manner scarcely short of the suicidal.

'It's really a dreadful place!' he exclaimed impulsively.
'I'm surprised, Dr Sutch, that you put up with it. Just a
little sweat—and possibly the loss of one or two menial
lives—could get the stuff down for you to ground level. And
there's no end of room for it in the rat-ridden pile.'

This had been a nervous and disagreeable speech—as
Charles Digitt knew even as he uttered it. But Dr Sutch,
who was holding open for him a door which might have
given access only to vacancy, received it impassively.

'The present muniment room,' he said, 'although
chargeable as being a shade eccentric, undoubtedly has its
convenience. It affords seclusion for unintermitted work. I
have very few vexatious interruptions while up here.'

At this, Charles took a civil leave of Dr Sutch and began
his descent. He was enough of a Digitt to tell himself that he
had just been made the recipient of a piece of damned
impertinence.

VII

IT WAS ON the following day, Tuesday, that Dr Sutch
sought an interview with his employer—or with his sec-
ondary employer, as the matter should perhaps be expressed,
bearing in mind his primary obligation to the Royal House
of Windsor. It was not altogether easy to achieve, since
Lord Ampersand had by this time come to regard his
learned hireling as an unmitigated pest. Lord Ampersand,
in whom a certain infirmity of purpose was sometimes to be
remarked, was on the verge of abandoning the notion that
there was money in Sutch—or in Sutch's burrowings in the
North Tower. He reminded himself that Skillet had on the
whole remained thoroughly sceptical about the entire project. And that Skillet was a smart chap was a fact that
sundry small family episodes, some of them not of the most
edifying sort, had borne in on him from time to time. Once
or twice he even meditated giving Sutch what he would
have termed a week's wages in lieu of notice, and bundling
him out of the castle. But Lady Ampersand had discouraged him in this drastic proposal, pointing out that such an
admission of fiasco might lead to ridicule on the part of her
husband's friends and neighbours. At this, Lord Ampersand, a sensitive man, had growled that he'd give the fellow
his head, and pay for his oats and hay at the Ampersand
Arms, for a further month. After that, they'd see.

The situation was the more annoying in that Sutch had
come to conceive himself as enjoying the freedom not only
of the North Tower but also of the castle as a whole. He

62

prowled around the place in an irritating way. On several occasions he had been known to accept a glass of port from Ludlow's pantry, gossiping with him the while. This was something which Lord Ampersand would sometimes do himself. He seldom made himself at all agreeable to his butler (as he did, it will be recalled, to the younger maid-servants), but he held feudal notions of what was proper from time to time in point of condescending behaviour to his more senior retainers. But in Dr Sutch the thing was shockingly unbecoming.

It was Ludlow who acted as an emissary. He presented himself to his master in the library (in which, in fact, Lord Ampersand had formed the habit of going virtually into hiding) and announced that Dr Sutch presented his compliments, and begged the favour of a few words with his lordship. So there was nothing for it. The man had to be let in. Dr Sutch entered, and made a remarkably formal bow.

'I hope I do not make a troublesome request,' he said. 'But I should be grateful if I might borrow your lordship's copy of Mackenzie's *The Castles of England*.'

'Ah, um,' Lord Ampersand said.

'It has excellent illustrations. And might I have, too, Clark's *Medieval Military Architecture*—which you will recall as being in two volumes—and Oman's *Art of War in the Middle Ages*?'

'Certainly, certainly, my dear sir.' Lord Ampersand felt awkwardly placed. As he lived in a castle, and as that castle had a substantial library, it seemed probable that he was indeed the proprietor of the works mentioned. And as he was at this moment sitting in the middle of that library, it might no doubt be expected of him that he could rise, take a few confident steps in the right direction, and produce Mackenzie, Clark and Oman as at the drop of a hat. But it was a dilemma not too difficult to resolve. 'Please take anything that interests you,' he said. 'The catalogue will guide you. That is, if there *is* a catalogue. And I do seem to remember one.'

Dr Sutch received these candid remarks with another bow.

'Certainly there is a catalogue, my lord, and I shall gratefully avail myself of it in a moment. But a word of explanation is perhaps necessary—if you are so obliging as to afford me the time.'

'Yes, of course. Do sit down.' Lord Ampersand, although disapproving of Sutch's manner of talking as it were out of an etiquette book, managed to be reasonably civil. 'Go right ahead.'

'You will remember the unfortunate events that succeeded at Treskinnick upon the death of the second marquess.'

'Ah, um.'

'The third marquess had never been favourably disposed towards Adrian Digitt, and had resented his father's harbouring him. When he came into the title he insisted that Adrian be never mentioned again in the family. He regarded him as one who had formed deplorable associations.'

'A bit uncharitable, eh? Natural, though. Those poets, and so forth.'

'The question is, how might this attitude have affected the disposal of Adrian Digitt's doubtless abundant literary remains? We have been acting on the supposition, I think it may be said, that they were simply neglected and then forgotten about. What has been brought together in the North Tower are essentially papers so treated. But there are other possibilities. I disregard one of these as barely conceivable. I refer, of course, to the third marquess's making a bonfire of everything that Adrian had left behind him. I would not disgrace myself, my lord, by believing that any Digitt could do quite that.'

Lord Ampersand could not repress a frown—or scowl. He disliked this orotundity; he disliked being continually addressed as 'my lord' as if by a flunkey; and he disliked what had certainly not been a tactful use of the word 'quite'. But he continued to restrain himself.

'Well,' he said, 'what more?'

'There is the possibility that the papers were very deliberately and carefully stored away; hidden, in fact, somewhere in the castle where no casual search would find them. By adopting such a course, the third marquess would effectively have got rid of papers which he probably regarded as scandalous, and at the same time would not have had on his conscience the actual destruction of what were, after all, valuable literary documents.'

'But they wouldn't have been all that valuable then, would they?' Lord Ampersand felt that he had stumbled upon an acute question. 'And we were quite well-off in those days—not scraping round after sixpences and shillings, you know. If the chap disliked the stuff, I'd expect him just to put a match to it. Unless matches hadn't yet been invented, that is.' This further precision of thought on his own part so pleased Lord Ampersand that he glanced at Dr Sutch almost with cordiality.

'Adrian Digitt's papers would even then have been widely regarded as valuable, my lord, even if not notably so in a pecuniary sense. Scholars and men of letters would have a great regard for them. You will remember the disfavour visited upon those among Byron's friends and associates who took it upon themselves to effect a similar, though limited, act of destruction.'

'Ah, um. But what has this got to do with fishing out books about castles and motes and places? Treskinnick was originally a mote, you know. Not a doubt about that. Once looked into it myself.'

Dr Sutch delivered himself of one of his grave bows, which was his way of being non-committal in face of his client's adventures into learning.

'Every ancient building of this character,' he said, 'has its hiding-places, the location of which may have passed out of memory. But exhaustive studies of military architecture contain many specific references to them. The volumes I seek may well do so in relation to Treskinnick, or at least may suggest fruitful lines of inquiry. One goes round measuring things.'

'The devil one does!'

'And takes soundings, and so on. And taps.'

'Good heavens!' Lord Ampersand was aghast. 'Do you mean you want to go tip-tap all through the castle? It would take you a month of Sundays, Dr Sutch. I never intended . . .'

'It may prove desirable. At the moment, however, I shall merely study the matter in the authorities I suggest.'

'Then go ahead, go ahead.' Lord Ampersand made a gesture comprehending the entire contents of the library, and at the same time jumped up and walked to the door. This tiresome interview had gone on quite as long as was tolerable. And it was once more time to walk the dogs. 'Good day to you,' he said. 'Leave you to it.' He bolted from the room.

It is to be presumed that Dr Sutch then worked on at his leisure. Certainly it was at an unusually late afternoon hour that he made his way back to the Ampersand Arms. He did so, moreover, by an unusual route: one perhaps affording particular opportunity for solitary meditation. If one descended to the shore by a path half a mile to the west of the castle and then turned east it was possible to round the castle over the tumble of rock beneath it, and then walk for a long way across firm sand to a point at which there was an answering ascent to the inn.

It was a cloudless evening, and there was still warmth from the declining sun. Dr Sutch, although no doubt aware of the beauties of external nature, and willing (like Byron) to find rapture on the lonely shore where none intrudes by the deep sea, moved slowly forward, as one lost in thought. From this abstraction he emerged only when actually beneath the castle and on the tricky stretch of his path. Here, indeed, he paused and looked up. There, high above his head, was the North Tower, scene of his present devoted services to scholarship. And there was that imbecile staircase. It would, of course, have been scarcely less hazardous had it made its way up another face of the building, since a fall to the inner ward would presumably be as fatal as one to the spot on which he now stood. But it was certainly more striking. The assumption had to be that the bird-watching Lord Ampersand had owned an eye for picturesque effect.

So thoughtfully, for the moment, was Dr Sutch's attention directed above that he was unaware of something happening below. Where immediately before there had been nothing but the bare face of the cliff there now stood a man of about Dr Sutch's own age. His sudden presence was completely mysterious. He wore a tin hat, had an electric torch strapped to his chest, and carried a small hammer.

'A beautiful evening,' this person said. 'How lucky I am to have emerged in time to view the sunset.'

'Emerged?' It has to be recorded that Dr Sutch repeated

the word blankly—but a moment later his powerful intelligence had grasped the situation. 'Sir,' he said courteously, 'am I to understand that you are a speleologist?'

'Most certainly.' The stranger must at once have gathered from Dr Sutch's ready command of this erudite word that he was in the presence of a fellow *savant*. 'My name,' he added, 'is Cave.'

'How do you do?' Dr Sutch refrained from making what, to Mr (or might it be Professor?) Cave, must have been a sadly familiar joke. 'I am Ambrose Sutch, and I may describe myself at present as archivist to the Marquess of Ampersand, under whose walls you are doubtless aware that we are standing now. May I say that it is a privilege to meet one in the great tradition of Monsieur Martel.'

'My dear sir, I should like so to think of myself. Martel was undoubtedly the founder of my science, such as it is. Before his time, the exploration of caverns, grottoes, and the subterranean regions of the earth in general was treated as a mere sport, or as affording material for writers of romance. You will recall *A Journey to the Centre of the Earth*. I confess that it a little touched my imagination as a boy.'

'Yes, indeed, Mr Cave. I myself remember being much struck by *Twenty Thousand Leagues under the Sea*. It fell short, however, of inducing me to make my career in submarines.'

Thus, under the rugged and louring mass of Treskinnick Castle, did these two learned persons agreeably converse. It transpired that Mr Cave actually intended to spend the night at the Ampersand Arms. He was engaged, he explained, on a very brief speleological survey of the region. It had proved so potentially rewarding that he proposed to make a more extended visit in a few weeks' time. Dr Sutch said a few words on his own manner of work, and the two men then fell into step together in the direction of their hostelry.

'Is there anything much close to Treskinnick itself?' Dr Sutch asked. 'You had the appearance, if I may say so, of having bobbed pretty well out of the bowels of the place.'

'Indeed, yes. Precisely so.' Mr Cave was delighted by this interest in his activities. 'There are several interconnecting caverns, the farther recesses of which must actually extend beneath the castle itself. It is my preliminary impression that they have been very little explored. The more accessible parts may have been utilized by smugglers at one time. And by pirates, if one cares to be romantic.'

'There was a Digitt in the late sixteenth century who was little better than a pirate, Mr Cave. Digitt, as you may know, is the family name of the Ampersands. And Narcissus Digitt was an associate of the celebrated Sir John Luttrell, whom it might be decent to describe as a corsair. It is curious to reflect that Narcissus may have anchored his craft, its hold full of booty, hard by in yonder cove.' As he made use of this poetical expression Dr Sutch made an equally poetical gesture to a spot a quarter of a mile ahead of them.

'He could have come right up to the castle, for the matter of that,' Mr Cave said. 'It is a point of some geological curiosity that there is a deep-water channel extending almost to the spot at which I had the pleasure of encountering you.'

'Most interesting! You and I might very well construct our own romance, don't you think? Shall we have a secret passage, for instance, winding up from the recesses of one of your caves into the very castle itself?'

'A splendid fancy! We entertain one another like schoolboys, do we not, my dear Dr Sutch? We must give Narcissus

Digitt a parrot and at the same time deprive him of a leg, so that he shall be a perfect Long John Silver.'

The Ampersand Arms was in sight before these two devoted scholars had tired of thus recreating themselves. They then had a drink together, and they dined together later on. Their talk, naturally, was much of the present state of knowledge and similar philosophical matters. These, in the poet Milton's phrase, were speculations high and deep. And it was perhaps only once or twice that each detected in the other a glance speculative in a different sense.

PART TWO

CRIMINAL INVESTIGATION AT TRESKINNICK CASTLE

VIII

SIR JOHN APPLEBY now appears on our scene. It is quite
fortuitously. He knows nothing whatever about Treskinnick Castle and its inhabitants: not even what a guide-book
or work of reference might have told him. He is on his way
to visit friends near St Ives, and has judged that he may be
going to arrive inconveniently early. So he has parked his
car, walked to the edge of the cliff, and observed a convenient declivity by which it is possible to reach a mile-long
beach. The beach is deserted; the sea is tranquil; it is a
good place for a walk. He scrambles down. Although
elderly, he remains of an active habit. It won't be at all
difficult to scramble up again. He will poke at seaweed,
examine shells, He rejoices at this peaceful prospect.

Yon castle hath a pleasant seat . . . Appleby has become
aware of Treskinnick in the middle distance, but he has
left his map in the car and is unable to identify it. Rather
vaguely, he compares it in his head with Tantallon in
Scotland. It is protected by the sea in just the same way.
But Tantallon is a ruin, and this place appears to be
inhabited. It even runs to a flag-staff, but no flag flies. So
perhaps the owner is not in residence. Appleby reflects
that, were his wife accompanying him on this present
expedition, they would undoubtedly assault the seemingly
impregnable pile and effect an entry—whether by bribery
or charm. Being alone, he will simply walk on, stare up at
the frowning mass of masonry, retrace his steps, and continue on his way.

And now he is aware of the North Tower, and of that mildly astonishing staircase. A bird—a gannet and not a temple-haunting martlet—is perched on top of it. The gannet rises, plunges, and disappears like a minute depth-charge into the sea. Had the gannet miscalculated, it would have bashed itself on rock. Appleby walks on, stops, does his gaping act. There is really nothing much to be seen. There is now sheer cliff more or less in front of his nose, a glimpse of the tower in violent foreshortening on top of it, a glimpse, too, of the skimpy wooden affair, which at its lower end must take some turn into an outer court of the castle. Appleby himself turns, and gazes out over the sea. An empty sea with no craft in sight. From the top of the tower behind him there must be a tremendous view. It is all very splendid, tranquil, silent.

The silence is broken. There is a rending sound, a crash, a rush of air past his face; then a momentary effect as of explosion and of debris falling and fallen everywhere in front of him. He has very nearly been killed.

And somebody *has* been killed. It is the staircase that has crashed. It lies in fragments all around him, and in the middle of the wreckage is sprawled the body of a man. The man's head is so disposed that there cannot be a moment's doubt as to his condition. He is as the gannet would have been had the gannet been careless about its fishing.

Appleby is never reckless; were he so, he would himself have been killed by one or another lethally disposed character long ago. For some seconds he stays put. There may be another instalment of the collapsed staircase to come. Then he risks it, advances, kneels down by the body. It doesn't take him long to confirm that the man is indeed dead.

There is another man. Quite suddenly, there is another

man—standing beside him and endeavouring to produce articulate speech. He succeeds only in mumbling. He is shocked, terrified. No doubt he is quite unused to this sort of thing. He can't be merely another casual stroller on the shore, since he is wearing a tin hat, has a large torch strapped to his chest, and carries tucked into a belt a variety of implements appropriate to some pursuit Appleby doesn't pause to identify.

'Did you see this happen?' Appleby asks.

'No—no, I didn't.' The man has achieved speech. 'I was in the cave. My name's Cave.'

Appleby (like Dr Sutch some weeks previously) may have found this homonymous information odd, but it wasn't something to pause on. Gently, he turned the body over.

'He's dead,' he said. 'Do you know him?'

The man called Cave gave a weak cry.

'It's Dr Sutch,' he said. 'From the castle.'

'Certainly from the castle. Are you familiar, sir, with these parts?'

'Slightly. Yes. I've been exploring them.'

'Very well. Go and get help. Contact the police, who will know what to do.'

'Is that the right thing?'

'Of course it is. My name is Sir John Appleby, and I've been a policeman myself. Tell them so; it may hurry them up. I shall stay here, since the body must not be abandoned. And get rid of all that gear, Mr Cave. It will only impede you. Although there's nothing to be done, it's only decent to make haste.'

'Yes, of course. How distressing this is!' Cave scrambled out of his impedimenta obediently. 'I'll have to go back for some way along the beach,' he said. 'It will take a little time.'

'Then do so. Tell them there will have to be a stretcher-party.'

'Yes, of course. What a hideous accident!'

'Quite so. And now, sir, be on your way.'

Thus urged, Mr Cave departed. Appleby produced a clean handkerchief and laid it over the dead man's face. Then he looked about him.

Mr Cave had emerged from a cave. Perhaps he had heard the crash, and had hurried out to investigate. He was presumably a habituated prowler in caves and pot-holes. It was an addictive pursuit. Or perhaps he was a person of some scientific standing in that sort of thing. But where was this particular cave? Appleby found it quite quickly, although its entrance was masked by an outcrop of rock. The sea ran into it through a channel so narrow that one could step over it. It appeared to be of a considerable depth, and on one side there was a broad platform of rock almost as smooth as a flagged pathway. Feeling some curiosity about its extent, Appleby possessed himself of Mr Cave's torch and made a brief exploration. He didn't venture far, since he was unwilling to abandon his wake over the unfortunate Dr Sutch's dead body.

Even so, he found something. As far as the beam of his torch could penetrate the cave was empty and showed no sign of being put to any use, save for one particular alone. Perhaps fifteen yards from the entrance, there lay a coil of rope. It was a long coil of rope, and extremely neatly disposed, so that at a glance it might have seemed an enormous rubber tyre. And beside it lay a coil of stout cord with a similar effect of precision. Hard-by a seaboard, there was nothing particularly out-of-the-way about these exhibits. Appleby looked at them in some perplexity, all the same. He stooped down and examined them. They were dry, and showed no sign of ever having been otherwise. They might, he told himself, have come straight from the shop.

He moved on a little farther. The cave took a turn, a second turn, and then bifurcated. It looked as if it might be part of an extensive system of caverns—a fact which would explain why the eponymous Mr Cave was interested in it. But there seemed to be no point in his proceeding farther himself. He turned back and regained the open air. Cave had disappeared, so he must be making reasonable haste. Appleby saw that he was in for rather a long vigil, nevertheless; in the end he might even have to ring up his friends in St Ives and announce a late arrival. Without disturbing Sutch's body, he poked about amid the debris of the staircase. It must have collapsed under the poor chap—and its condition had plainly been such that this was not wholly surprising. Much of the woodwork was actually rotten. It occurred to Appleby that if Dr Sutch had been in any manner an employee of whoever owned the castle, awkward claims for compensation might result from the fatality. The staircase must have been eccentrically hazardous when first constructed; if you had hired a man to go up and down it in its latter-day condition you were risking being booked for trouble.

Appleby walked away from the cliff and along the shore until the upper ranges of the tower came into full view again. If it wasn't exactly a ruin, it was getting on that way. It ended off in crumbling crenellations behind which presumably lay a flat roof; there were bricked-up windows or apertures most of the way up; only the topmost range showed glass and appeared to be in reasonable repair. Not much more of the castle was visible from where he stood, and in what he could see there was no sign of life. He was probably too far off to hear anything in the nature of commotion. But commotion there must surely be. If there had been anybody at all even in the recesses of the ramifying building, that resounding crash must have made itself heard. And one almost had to suppose that Dr Sutch had ended his life screaming. It was a disquieting thought, and prompted Appleby to take another look at the dead man. On the late Dr Sutch's feet a weight of something like twenty stones had habitually reposed. That might be a factor in what happened.

From the castle to the spot on which Appleby stood there appeared to be no direct descent. But by whatever route was practicable somebody could come down as quickly as Cave could go up—supposing it to be to the castle that Cave had betaken himself. So it was beginning to be a little odd that nobody had appeared. For an alarm there must have been, and one would expect rapid investigation to follow.

But now, in fact, somebody was approaching, and not from the direction in which Cave had gone off. It was a man in evening dress—a circumstance of which, at eleven o'clock in the morning, there could be only one explanation. The owner of the castle must hold somewhat outmoded views on how it was proper for upper servants to attire themselves right round the clock. The outfit plainly included shoes not well adapted to moving over rock, and this was perhaps why the newcomer was visibly in a bad temper as he came up.

'Good-morning,' Appleby said. 'Are you from the castle?'

'Yes, I am. There's been an accident, and his lordship saw it happen. He has told me to come down and take a look. Oh, my God!' The man had seen Dr Sutch.

'Yes,' Appleby said. 'He's dead. It was a tremendous drop.' He was reflecting that if his lordship (whoever he might turn out to be) had actually seen Dr Sutch fall in ruin (as the poem says) to the gulfs below, he had given a rather casual instruction to his butler. But in such exigencies as the present the aristocracy no doubt have their own manner of address. 'What castle is this?' he asked briskly. 'And who is your employer?'

'This is Treskinnick Castle, and it's the seat of the Marquess of Ampersand.' The butler paused. 'And my name,' he added with dignity, 'is Ludlow.'

'Well, Mr Ludlow, this is a sad business, as you can see, and I fear there is nothing we can do. You had better go back and tell Lord Ampersand that Dr Sutch is undoubtedly dead. Tell him, too, that I am awaiting the arrival of the police to deal with the matter. Lord Ampersand won't have heard of me. But tell him that my name is Sir John Appleby.'

'You're right that he'll never have heard of it,' Ludlow said. 'But I have. It comes of reading *The Times*.' He paused after making this surprising remark. 'And very proper it is,' he added more surprisingly still, 'that inquiries are being made by Scotland Yard.'

'My dear Mr Ludlow, you are getting this wrong. I've had nothing to do with Scotland Yard for several years. I am here simply by chance, and am a complete stranger to your situation, as you might have gathered from the inquiries I had to make about my whereabouts. It is the local police who will deal with this fatality.' On this Appleby nodded dismissively. But then (and fatally) a start of professional curiosity possessed him. 'Only,' he said, 'just be so good as to tell me why, in your opinion, it is proper that inquiries should be made. Are you suggesting that there is some situation at Treskinnick which might lead you to suppose that Dr Sutch has been the victim of foul play? It is a very serious thing, you must be aware, even to hint at anything of that kind.'

'I wouldn't say that, Sir John.' Ludlow seemed unperturbed by the severity of Appleby's admonition. 'But queer things have been happening. There's no doubt about that.'

'I see. Well, just who was this Dr Sutch? I know his name, by the way, because a certain Mr Cave knows it; Mr Cave was here when the thing happened, and has gone for help. Are you acquainted with Mr Cave?'

'I never heard of him. He wouldn't be a man who goes wandering along the beach in a thing like a miner's hat?'

'Yes, that is Mr Cave, all right.'

'Then I saw him talking to this Sutch a couple of days ago, not far from the castle. It was when I had to take the dogs out, his lordship having had his touch of gout. As for Sutch, he has been around for some time, looking over family papers and the like for his lordship. Yes, he's been at it for months. A peering-around sort of man. And he'd come into my quarters and be too familiar to be quite comfortable, if you know what I mean. Come in and chat as if he was the family.'

'So he has been living in the castle?'

'His lordship wouldn't have him, and we put him up at the Ampersand Arms. Supposed just to work up there in the North Tower, he was—which is where the papers are, and where he has fallen from. But he was going all over the castle, all the same—and in a very presuming way, to my mind. Measuring and tapping and all that.'

'*Tapping*, Mr Ludlow?'

'The panelling and the like. Looking for secret chambers, he told me. What do you make of that?'

'I'm not in a position to make anything of it at all, Mr

Ludlow. I suppose confidential papers might be stowed away in such a place. But it's no business of mine.' Appleby thought that this might sound unnecessarily snubbing. 'It's different with yourself, no doubt. You must carry a great deal of responsibility at Treskinnick.'

'That I do.' The Marquess of Ampersand's butler, who had been disposed to treat Appleby (doubtless a mere knight bachelor) with a just reserve, was clearly gratified by this last remark, and showed signs of becoming conversable. And although extended chat would have been unseemly when conducted more or less across a dead body, Appleby couldn't resist one further question. 'Those queer things that have been happening,' he said. 'How would you describe them?'

'Well, there's been more coming and going on that crazy staircase than seems reasonable to me. And the key to what they call the muniment room—up there at the top of it—disappearing and reappearing again. And lights up there in the small hours. Flickering lights—like it might have been with the old wreckers giving their evil signals.'

'I see.' Appleby was impressed by this unexpected start of historical imagination on the part of Lord Ampersand's rather wooden butler. 'Well, there won't be anything more of that kind now. Except that surely the tower must have an internal staircase?'

'Blocked up for centuries, that has been. That's why the last marquess built the wooden affair. And he did it on the cheap, I'd imagine. If it was my place to imagine anything, that's to say, Sir John. Near-going, all the Digitts have been, when not squandering their money on gambling and harlots.'

'I'm sorry to hear it.' Ludlow, it struck Appleby, must be distinctly upset—and presumably it was by the late fatality.

He would scarcely otherwise have permitted himself so distinctly unfavourable a view of the Digitt *mores*. 'But I'm detaining you, Mr Ludlow. You'd better be getting back to the castle. I shall stay here until the police arrive.'

Ludlow departed, and quite soon the police did turn up. They were accompanied by the local doctor, and they announced that an ambulance could be brought along the beach to within a hundred yards of the dead man. Appleby realized that, despite this take-over by authority, he couldn't now himself simply make off. If one has the misfortune to be the first person to stumble upon a corpse, one can't do that—not even if one is a retired Commissioner of Metropolitan Police. He'd have to stay put for a time, and have what he had to say got down in writing. But meantime, if he wanted to, he could talk to Mr Cave, since Mr Cave had returned to the scene of the accident. Perhaps the police had insisted on this. Or perhaps Mr Cave was just curious. Appleby went up to him.

'I'm afraid you are missing your lunch,' he said, 'just as I'm going to do. Are you staying somewhere in the neighbourhood?'

'I'm at the Ampersand Arms, about two miles away. It's not much of a pub.'

'I've gathered that the dead man had been living there, and not at the castle. I suppose that explains your knowing who he was.'

'Yes, of course. That's to say, Dr Sutch and I met by chance some weeks ago, when I was down here on a preliminary survey. We dined together, and had a little talk. I haven't met him since, and I didn't gather a great deal about him.'

'Naturally not.' Mr Cave, it seemed to Appleby, had put a certain effect of nervous disclaimer into this last remark.

'You would each of you gather something of the other's interests and present occasions: no more than that.'

'Exactly. Sutch was engaged on some research into the Digitts' family papers. And I was here because I am by profession a speleologist. We simply chatted about these things.'

'It seems that he was expected to work in a room at the top of that tower, and to come and go by that remarkable staircase. Did he express any apprehensiveness about that?'

'No, I don't think so. No, I can't recall that he did.'

Appleby glanced curiously at Mr Cave, not a reliable or even wholly veracious man. Perhaps he was too scared to be either. Certainly at what was, after all, no more than a hint of interrogation he was turning oddly agitated and wary. It was perhaps unfortunate that he was conscious of conversing with a policeman—and with a top policeman, at that. It was something—Appleby knew from long experience—calculated to render the most innocent persons uneasy.

'That's an interesting cave,' he said, changing the subject. 'I took a glance round it while you were away. It isn't you who has stored that coil of rope in it, I suppose?'

'Rope?' For a moment Cave looked quite blank. 'Ah, yes—I remember what you must be speaking of. I noticed it myself, that is to say. But, no—of course not. Why should it be?'

'It occurred to me that it might be connected with climbing equipment, and that you might make use of it on the cliff-face here and there. No doubt it has something to do with the fisher-folk round about.'

'That must be it. I wonder, Sir John, whether the police wish to detain me? To detain me further, I mean. After all, the accident was over and done with by the time I came on the scene, was it not.'

'I suppose it might be expressed that way. You certainly emerged from the cave to find a dead man. And myself, of course. Incidentally, I rather want to get away fairly soon too. So I think I can promise, Mr Cave, that we shall both be allowed to go our ways within the next fifteen minutes.'

'That will be rather a relief, I confess. I fear I am not habituated to this sort of thing. Not, of course, that I don't wish to be other than helpful in any way I can.'

'Of course not,' Appleby said. 'But unless you happen to know the people at the castle, and feel that you can be of use to them in any way . . .'

'Oh, no. Nothing of the kind! I mean that Lord Ampersand and his family are quite unknown to me. Even by repute, I am ashamed to say.'

'My dear Mr Cave, your position is precisely mine.' Appleby offered this, rather vaguely, as a composing remark, since Mr Cave again appeared to be a little agitating himself. 'I don't think I've ever heard of them. They are probably prominent in these parts. But not, perhaps, in the public life of the country, shall we say. Ah! Here is the Inspector coming to speak to us. We'll be off in no time now. I can assure you of that.'

IX

OVER THE NEXT few days the mysterious affair at Treskinnick Castle (for it did seem to hold an element of mystery, although a small one) intermittently troubled the conscience of Sir John Appleby. To be more precise, he was disturbed by the thought that nobody else was likely to suspect that the death of Dr Sutch had, so to speak, any inwardness to itself at all.

But in this he turned out to be wrong. On the day before he was due to make his homeward journey he received a telephone call from a man called Brunton, who had been a close colleague of his a good many years previously. Brunton had long ago departed from Scotland Yard, and was now a Chief Constable.

'Appleby?' Brunton said. 'Sorry to run you to earth, but here's an odd thing. I've been brought papers about some fellow who got himself killed at Treskinnick Castle the other day. And it seems you were on the spot. Odd coincidence.'

'And sinister, no doubt.'

'I don't think I'd go as far as to say that—or not at this stage.' Indications of amusement came over the line. 'It looks like an open-and-shut affair—and vaguely Lord Ampersand's fault for not keeping some crazy structure or other in reasonable repair. But they're uneasy about it.'

'What do you mean by "they"? Are you talking about your own people?'

'Well, no—not exactly. A member of the family, as a matter of fact.'

'One of the Dodg'ems, or whatever they're called?'

'That's right—the Digitts. I expect you know some of them.'

'Absolutely not.'

'At least one of them knows you.'

'Nonsense, Brunton.'

'Call it by repute. And she wants you to look into the thing.'

'My dear man, just because some member of the public . . .'

'You mustn't call a peer's daughter just a member of the public. It's disrespectful.' The sound of mirth renewed itself.

'Don't be an ass, Brunton.' Appleby was not amused. 'It would be completely irregular for me to meddle with the thing. I no longer have so much as a warrant card.'

'You can't expect Lady Grace Digitt to be impressed by a technicality like that. She says she's read your evidence before that blessed Commission, and been most impressed by it.'

'I see. If not a member of the public, at least a public woman.'

'Quite so. A strong-minded woman. And has her father under her thumb, if you ask me.'

'I don't ask. I'm devoid of all curiosity in the matter. Just what is this Lady Grace uneasy about?'

'There you are!' Once more there was mirth in the Chief Constable's office. 'She's not very precise, as a matter of fact.'

'Then invite her to be so, and in the presence of a respectably senior member of your Force.'

'Look here, Appleby. I know you can't have been on the scene of this affair for much more than a bare hour. But I don't doubt you were looking about you in the old familiar way—and keeping your ears open as well. Was there anything, anything at all, that made you a shade uneasy yourself?'

'Ah!' Silently to himself, Appleby acknowledged that this put him awkwardly on the spot. 'I can, as it happens, mention one very small circumstance that puzzled me. So take it down, and hand it to your fellow dealing with this grand Sutch mystification. I just chanced to notice . . .'

'Appleby, you can't ride away from the thing like that. You could call in on your way home, couldn't you? I'll have my man waiting at the castle to brief you. Craig's his name. Level-headed and unassuming officer.'

'Very well.' To what he tried to think of as his own surprise, Appleby had given in. 'But tell him to be at the local pub. I believe it's called the Ampersand Arms. If he then succeeds in dragging me to Treskinnick Castle, he'll be a notably persuasive man.'

'Absolutely fair. About noon tomorrow?'

'About noon.'

'Right! Good-bye.'

Appleby put down the receiver. He wasn't pleased with himself, and his wife wouldn't be pleased with him either. She had invited the Birch-Blackies to dinner that evening. Appleby didn't greatly care for the Birch-Blackies. So Judith would suspect him of wantonly evasive action if he didn't turn up when promised. She might even make ribald remarks about the charms of Lady Grace Digitt.

These domestic cares didn't stay with Appleby for long. Nor, for that matter, did he put in much time thinking about the late Dr Sutch, since he still knew far too little about him to make any exercise of the kind at all profitable. What he did find himself meditating as he drove through

Cornwall on the following morning was something that no longer effectively existed: the fatal staircase itself. It had, for a start, one peculiar property. Take it away (and it *had* been taken away), and access to the chamber at the head of it became impossible to achieve except at the expense of much time and effort. Nobody could claw his way up that tower. Skilled men could no doubt drive into one face of it or another supports or appliances enabling some sort of ladder to be progressively built up. But it would be a risky employment. And if the vanished staircase were to be replaced (perhaps an unlikely event) quite an elaborate and costly scaffolding would be required for the purpose. Probably a fire brigade had been called in—but no fire brigade was going to tie up its vital equipment in a big way while Lord Ampersand reorganized the conduct of what appeared to be genealogical researches. It was true, of course, that once a couple of steeplejacks had been thus hoisted to the top, they could readily enough fix up some device for ascending and descending in a tolerably safe, even if hair-raising manner. But one essential consequence of what had happened was that the so-called muniment room at Treskinnick Castle had been put out of commission for some time.

There was more to the North Tower and its staircase than this. It was a set-up positively inviting a play of the imagination—and of a macabre imagination, were one feeling that way inclined. If at Treskinnick a man were to set himself to evolving anything in the way of dark villainy or miching malicho, he would be unenterprising if he didn't build that staircase into his scenario.

This perhaps fanciful thought was still lurking in Appleby's mind when he reached the Ampersand Arms and contacted Inspector Craig. About Inspector Craig you could tell at a glance that there was nothing fanciful at all. Nor was he a respecter of persons to the extent of being put out at being suddenly thrust into the society of a retired Commissioner. He was carrying a notebook in which all matters held relevant to the death of Dr Sutch were doubtless already ranged in an orderly manner.

'We'll go elsewhere', Appleby said, without getting out of his car. 'So get in and direct me. To another pub three or four miles away. Where we can rely on the beer, if possible.'

Craig did as he was told—and certainly without being mystified. Newspaper interest in the late Sutch must have been lively during the past few days. And while it was unlikely that any reporter was still lingering around, the Ampersand Arms would be his most likely haunt if he were. Any such hopeful snapper up of belated intelligence would unquestionably regard the arrival of Sir John Appleby on the scene as being worth a paragraph. Ludlow, it was true, would be unlikely to come across it in *The Times*. But elsewhere it might be made quite a thing of.

'The next on the right will take us to the Cornish Elephant,' Craig said presently. 'A silly name, and I can't vouch for the beer. But they do have excellent cider.'

So they settled for the Cornish Elephant, and were provided with sandwiches and cider in a deserted saloon bar.

'I hope,' Appleby said, 'that your Chief Constable made it clear to you that I don't know those people at Treskinnick from Adam.'

'Yes, sir; he played quite fair there.' Craig, a man of confident address, was inoffensively amused—and (what was important) clearly by no means resentful of Appleby's irregular appearance on his pitch. 'I think he felt you could cope with Lord Ampersand.'

'Does Lord Ampersand need coping with?'

'He's perhaps a little difficult to pin down. Not very deep, I'd say—but of course you never know. Certainly not like Lord Skillet.'

'And who is Lord Skillet?'

'He's the heir, and I don't know that I'd trust him. And the same goes for Mr Charles Digitt.'

'And who, in turn, is he?'

'A nephew—and the next heir after Lord Skillet.'

'I rather gathered from Mr Brunton that the only person to be uneasy about this affair is a daughter called Lady Grace. But now, Inspector, you seem to be weaving a net of suspicion here and there round this whole noble family. Is that so?'

'Well, Sir John, I have been beginning to wonder. Somehow or other, I can't get my mind away from that staircase.'

'Ah, now you interest me. I've been feeling the same way. Something pat and obvious about the accident that doesn't ring quite true. There's a kind of challenge in it.'

'Exactly, sir. Like those things about alibis in the detective stories. If somebody tipped Sutch off the staircase, that somebody has the most tremendous alibi that ever was.'

'Not quite strictly an alibi, is it, Mr Craig?'

'Well, no. But you see what I mean. The moment the staircase fell . . .'

'. . . the murderer was imprisoned in the scene of his crime. He'd effectively isolated himself, and couldn't possibly get away. And as you found no cowering miscreant, I assume, when you got somebody up there, it follows that there *was* no murder. It's a point that Sherlock Holmes would have established at once. You were quite right, by the way, about this cider.'

'I'm glad you like it, Sir John. I like it myself a lot more

90

than I like the conclusion we seem forced to accept. Looked at rationally, the affair gives no hint of being other than an accident. And I hate mere baseless hunches.'

'They can certainly land one in a mess, Mr Craig. What about this Lady Grace Digitt? Why does she imagine there was a crime, if that's what's in her head? She can't be requiring you to suspect her parents or brother or sister or cousin or whomsoever of hideous wickedness.'

'No, that's not possible—or only on some entirely extravagant hypothesis. But I think she feels some member of her family—or at least of the household—may be suspected, and that the situation ought to be cleared up so as to obviate anything of the sort. I think she may talk about it to you as she won't do to me.'

'I can't think why.'

'Reputation, Sir John. Simply reputation.' Craig presented this explanation with amused assurance, and as a man who knows he occasions no umbrage. Quite a good chap to work with, Appleby thought.

'Have you a ghost of a notion, Craig, why anybody should want to kill Sutch? He sounds like some perfectly harmless drudge.'

'All I seem to gather is that his work involved issues that might lead to family friction, even animosity. That certainly seems to be at the back of Lady Grace's mind. And even Lord Ampersand can be felt to have a dim sense of it.'

'What about Lady Ampersand? What sort of woman is she?'

'I don't think she could be called very well-informed or intelligent. But she strikes me as a sensible woman—these limitations allowed for.'

'You know about the man called Cave?'

'He's on the record, of course.' Craig tapped his

notebook, which he hadn't yet ventured to open. 'He was your other contact, in a way, was he not?' Craig looked shrewdly at Appleby. 'The Chief Constable said you had some small thing on your mind, sir. It wouldn't have been about this Cave?'

'There in one, Inspector.' Appleby nodded a very senior man's approval. 'Cave didn't say much to me, and I wasn't thinking of him as more than on the fringe of the affair. But what he did say included a lie. He said he'd talked to Sutch only once—some weeks before, and when they'd run up against each other by chance, and dined together. But the butler, Ludlow, says he saw them confabulating—apparently in the open air—a long time after that.'

'It couldn't be Ludlow who was telling the lie?'

'Certainly it might.' Appleby's approval was again evident. 'Ludlow might conceivably have some motive of his own for suggesting that those two were in some sort of conspiracy. But it's very conjectural, Inspector.'

'So it is.'

'And what I caught Cave out in may be quite without significance. He was suddenly in the presence of violent death—and of a policeman. I could see that it all frightened him very much. He'd have an irrational impulse to dissociate himself from the dead man in every way. You know the strange and irresponsible fashion in which people do behave in that sort of crisis. Our work would be very much easier if they didn't.'

'A true word, sir. I think we ought to get on to Cave again.'

'Yes, I think you ought.'

'He was in the cave at the bottom of the cliff, I gather, and came out immediately the thing happened?'

'Well, yes. I supposed him to have heard the crash. But

he might have emerged a minute or two before I became aware of him. You've been in the cave?'

'Of course, Sir John.' Inspector Craig said this a shade stiffly.

'That rope and cord were still there?'

'Yes.'

'Notice anything about them?'

'They hadn't been thrown down in a hurry.'

'Exactly. It was an almost finical chap who disposed them the way they were. A fisherman would wind them into a coil, no doubt—but not quite like that. Or so it struck me, Craig '

'Would you call this Cave finical?'

'Good question. Yes. A sort of light-weight scientific mind. Leave things tidy in the lab.'

'Cave might have been depositing the stuff there.'

'Certainly he might. Or have gone in to retrieve it—and bolted out when the staircase tumbled. If he'd just been up to something shady, it would account for his funk.'

'It seems, Sir John, that he departed from that pub almost as soon as he'd got back to it. We'd taken his statement, of course, for what it seemed worth. But we'll put him on our list again.' Inspector Craig opened his notebook at last. 'And now, sir, may I tell you everything I've gathered?'

'Another half-pint of the cider, and go ahead.'

And in the most orderly way, Craig proceeded to tell Appleby much—but not all—that the reader already knows about the Ampersands and their concerns.

X

At Treskinnick Castle Appleby was received not by
Lord Ampersand (who was declared to be walking the
dogs) but by Lord Ampersand's elder daughter, Lady
Grace Digitt. Both the Chief Constable and Inspector
Craig had made remarks preparing Appleby for something
of the kind. Of the crisis that had befallen this noble household Lady Grace had more or less taken charge.

Her younger sister, Lady Geraldine, was also present.
She might have been described, perhaps, as in attendance,
since her contribution to the discussion mainly took the
form of affirmative nods. If she wanted at times to shake her
head in a strongly negative fashion (and Appleby somehow
suspected that she did) she steadily repressed any such
impulse. She managed to give an impression of being ready
to pounce, all the same. If Grace was indeed a clever public
woman, Geraldine was perhaps the same thing a shade
manqué.

'The man Sutch,' Grace said, 'came to us on the recommendation of my brother, Skillet.'

'Ah, yes.' Appleby gave an affirmative nod of his own.
'Lord Skillet's name has been mentioned to me by Inspector Craig.'

'No doubt, Sir John. And it is my fear that my brother
was deceived.'

'Although he is very clever,' Geraldine said helpfully.
'Archie is very clever indeed.'

'It may be so, Geraldine.' Grace had frowned slightly.

'But it is my point that Sutch was a most undesirable person, who has ended by occasioning us very considerable embarrassment. That wretched staircase was undoubtedly in very poor repair—but Sutch, nevertheless, must have been uncommonly careless on it. It was thoughtless of him, to say the least. My father will be most distressed if unfavourable comment is passed on the situation at, say, the inquest. I shall speak to the coroner about it beforehand, and have no doubt that he will be discreet.'

'It is a pleasant confidence to have, Lady Grace.'

'But others may not be. The position is extremely vexatious, and may become even more so if it begins to be suspected that there was some sinister background to the affair.'

'Do you yourself feel that there was something of the kind?'

'In a sense, yes. And my sister agrees with me. That is so, Geraldine, is it not?'

Geraldine gave her nod.

'It is my sense that Sutch was an unprincipled person, and that he had involved himself in intrigue.'

'In intrigue?' Appleby looked properly puzzled and distressed. 'The term is commonly taken to suggest something in the nature of a conspiracy between two or more persons. Are you saying that you believe that to be the state of the case?'

'Decidedly.'

'Then with whom was Dr Sutch conspiring? It can hardly, I take it, have been with a member of your family or household.'

'Of course not—and I fear I can give no helpful answer to your question. But one thing it is necessary to say. Whatever was going on did tend to exercise an exacerbating or

95

irritant effect upon certain members of the family. They were set a little at odds, shall we say. And this, Sir John, is the occasion of my appealing to you. If the mystery is not resolved in a clear-headed way, baseless suspicions may be aroused.'

'That would be most unfortunate, of course.' Appleby had a sense that things were turning uncommonly odd at this interview. 'But *is* there necessarily any mystery? You have just been saying that Dr Sutch was careless, and unhappily with fatal consequences.'

'I am not quite satisfied as to that.' For the first time, Grace Digitt hesitated. 'There is, you see, this background to the affair in those extremely valuable papers. I have been making inquiries about them.'

'Ah, yes—the papers. Mr Craig has some sort of note about that. But perhaps you can give me a fuller view of that aspect of the affair. If, indeed, it can conceivably have anything to do with Dr Sutch's death. The police, you know, and for that matter I myself, are concerned solely with that.'

'No doubt. I have to confess that I was not well-informed about the papers once possibly in the possession of Adrian Digitt. It is not my sort of thing. I was slow to appreciate the point that this merely literary material might be very valuable indeed.'

'And so well worth intriguing about.' It was Geraldine who unexpectedly offered this contribution to the debate.

'Exactly so. My sister makes the vital point, Sir John. Skillet at one time talked about them in such a vein, although he has not latterly done so. I was inclined to discount his remarks.'

'Archie, you see,' Geraldine said as if by way of explanatory aside, 'talks a good deal.'

'It may be said,' Grace went on, 'that we were in a weak

situation. We had no certainty that these papers existed at
all, whether at Treskinnick or anywhere else. Sutch, if he
came upon them, would have been in a position to misap-
propriate the lot. But to dispose of them he would presumably have required accomplices of some sort. It is in this
context that I speak of the possibility of intrigue.'

'I see.' Appleby paused, aware that Grace Digitt was no
fool—and aware, too, that here was a point at which caution was required. 'But suppose we make a contrary supposition. Suppose Dr Sutch to have been an honest
man . . .'

'As it is incumbent upon us to do, so long as we lack
evidence to disprove it.' Predictably (Appleby told himself)
Geraldine had pounced at last.

'Quite so, Lady Geraldine. So let me continue. Imagine
Dr Sutch to have found the papers, and to have taken them
straight to Lord Ampersand. Might there then have been
any dispute as to their ownership?'

'Indeed there might.' Grace spoke without hesitation. 'I
have discussed the issue on the telephone with our family
solicitor, Sir John. It is his opinion that the papers,
regarded as physical objects merely, might be adjudged to
be the property of my father. But since they have never
been published, the copyright in them continues in being
indefinitely, and may at this moment be the legal property
of some legitimate descendant of Adrian Digitt's, supposing such a person to exist. So your question is answered,
Sir John. There might well be dispute about the matter. It
would, of course, be a disgraceful thing.'

Appleby didn't quite see that it need be a disgraceful
thing. But he did see that a point of substance had emerged
about those hypothetical Ampersand Papers.

'Lady Grace,' he asked, 'do you yourself possess any

information as to whether or not a descendant of Adrian Digitt's is alive today?'

'I have discussed the question with a cousin, Charles Digitt. As it happens, he is staying at the castle now. But I first raised the problem with him a considerable time ago, when this fuss about Adrian Digitt arose. He appeared at that time disinclined to treat it seriously, and had nothing to say about it. Indeed, I cannot say that he was wholly civil to me. But now, and no doubt as a consequence of this shocking affair, he has been more communicative. We have a distant relation, an elderly woman named Deborah Digitt, who lives at Budleigh Salterton. Charles believes her to be Adrian Digitt's great-granddaughter, and his only living descendant. So the copyright of which we have been speaking may well be her property.'

'Might not the papers be her property too—and actually in her possession? She would appear to be the natural person to have inherited them. Has inquiry been made of this Miss Digitt?'

'It shall be made, of course.' Grace said this grimly. 'We haven't got round to it yet.'

'I see.' Appleby paused for moment. 'Allow me, Lady Grace, to put what is admittedly an extremely bizarre suggestion to you. Suppose that the papers were here at Treskinnick, and that the copyright was Miss Deborah Digitt's. Might she not feel that the tidy thing, as it were, would be that the papers themselves should be in her possession too? After all, she might well believe that she had a moral, and even legal, right to them. Might she not have decided to simplify matters, as it were, by entering into what you call an intrigue with Dr Sutch?'

There was a moment's silence, during which Appleby had the satisfaction of seeing that he had produced an absurdity (as it must surely be) that the competent Grace Digitt hadn't thought of. Oddly enough, it looked as if Geraldine had. For this time she had given a nod of a peculiar character, rather as if acknowledging that here was a glimpse of the obvious.

'We have no reason to suppose,' Grace said a little coldly, 'that Miss Digitt, although living, indeed, in an obscure situation, is other than a person of unblemished character.'

'Nor have we of Dr Sutch, Lady Grace, although his was no doubt an obscure situation too. I only wished to bring home to your sister and yourself the curious manner in which suspicions may ramify, when once embarked upon. I wonder whether it will be possible for me to have some conversation with your father?'

'I see him coming through the main gate now.' Grace was standing by a window. 'And Skillet with him.'

'And the dogs,' Geraldine said.

'Sir John is unlikely to wish to converse with *them*, Geraldine,' Grace said severely.

'I suppose not, Grace. At least we haven't given the dogs a bad name.'

This unexpected witticism was not well received by the elder daughter of the Ampersands. Grace walked to the door.

'My sister and I will now withdraw, Sir John,' she said with a touch of *hauteur*, 'and I shall ask my father and brother to join you.'

So Appleby was left for some minutes to his own devices. At least he no longer felt himself to be in any false position. Here was a mystery of sorts, and he had made his life among such things. He was quite prepared to assume the full mantle of the law, and sort these Digitts out. It was true that he hadn't developed (as he had occasionally done in the past) a rather instant insight into the state of the case. If Dr Sutch had been murdered, it was difficult to see just how. It was still more difficult to see in all this stuff about Adrian Digitt's remains anything that could have quite the weight to precipitate a crime of such a sort. The unfortunate Dr Sutch, indeed, had been precipitated, but there was still very little reason to suppose that he hadn't, so to speak, precipitated himself. At least there had been nobody to give him a lethal shove.

Or had there been? Why not? Why *not*? Just suppose that . . .

But no. It was impossible. Thinking back hard, Appleby told himself that what had glimmered in his mind just wouldn't work. The clock was against it. And, in any case, it was utterly improbable that, in such a situation, anybody would pause . . .

The door opened. Lord Ampersand and his son, Lord Skillet, entered the room.

XI

'It must have been the helicopter,' Lord Ampersand said.

'The helicopter?' Appleby repeated, at a loss before this abrupt announcement.

'Yes, the helicopter. It must have been that. I've been turning over one thing and another. And that's it.'

'You will observe, Sir John,' Lord Skillet said, 'that my father has been addressing his mind to our problem.'

'Properly so,' Appleby returned drily, and made a mental note that the heir of the Ampersands was one given to irony and perhaps malice. 'But just what helicopter, Lord Ampersand?'

'Well, you know, they're around a great deal. The naval station has the things. Police borrowed one, as a matter of fact, to land a fellow up there on the North Tower.'

'Did they, indeed?' It surprised Appleby that Inspector Craig had not reported this obvious manoeuvre.

'Confounded nuisance they can be, my dear sir.' Lord Ampersand appeared to remain a little vague as to Appleby's identity. 'Make the devil of a racket at times. But what I remembered, you see, was a kinsman of mine who was a fighter pilot during the war. Resourceful chap. Discovered how to cope with those buzz-things. He'd come up behind them, and just touch a fin, or whatever it was to be called, with his wing-tip. And down it would go into the English Channel.'

'Lord Ampersand, are you suggesting that this is how Dr Sutch met his end?'

'That's right. Bit of a lark, I suppose. High-spirited fellows. Of course, the chap mayn't have noticed Sutch crawling around. Unfortunate, eh?'

'Decidedly so.'

'Or the catastrophe,' Lord Skillet said, 'may have been wholly inadvertent. The helicopter simply flew too near to that staircase, and the mere turbulence from the rotors brought it down. As my father says, that's it. So we needn't trouble ourselves further.'

'I fear we shall have to trouble ourselves quite a lot further, Lord Skillet.' Appleby accompanied this expression of opinion with a stony glance at Archie before turning back to his father. 'Are you saying, Lord Ampersand, that there *was* a helicopter?'

'It stands to reason, doesn't it? Otherwise it couldn't have happened that way.' Lord Ampersand paused on this triumph of logic. 'But I quite accept what my son has to say. Pure accident, and so on.'

'Lord Ampersand, it appears from the police report that you yourself actually *saw* the staircase collapse . . .

'Perfectly true. It was quite worrying, my dear Sir Robert.'

'John. Do you now assert that you also saw a helicopter—and heard it as well?'

'Well now, I can't say that.' Lord Ampersand had the air of a patient man meeting some merely captious criticism. 'As I say, the things are around a great deal. It's so usual that one ceases to notice them. But the staircase giving way like that wasn't usual at all. In fact, I never saw it happen before. So of course I was aware of that.'

'As always,' Lord Skillet said, 'my father is the soul of lucidity. I look forward to his explaining the affair to our local naval commander.'

'That, I judge, is unlikely to happen.' Appleby wondered whether Lord Skillet was quite as frivolous as he appeared determined to represent himself. 'We must put your father's theory out of our heads, for the simple reason that I myself know quite positively that there was no aircraft of any kind around. I was down there at the foot of the cliff, you see, when the staircase fell, and Dr Sutch with it.' Appleby paused on this long enough to see that he had disconcerted his auditory. It was odd that this piece of information seemed to come as a surprise to these people. Or was that the position? There was nothing astonishing in the fact that Lord Ampersand was a good deal less on the ball than his daughters. But what about his son? Appleby found himself wondering whether Lord Skillet was a man who—habitually and, as it were, by routine—faked his reactions to whatever turned up.

'How disagreeable for you,' Lord Skillet said. 'Sutch was rather an old tortoise in a way. And the helicopter, like Aeschylus's eagle, might have dropped him plumb on your head.'

It is unlikely that this somewhat strained piece of classical lore meant much to Lord Ampersand. But Lord Ampersand nodded appreciatively, all the same. He probably held his heir in high regard, at least intellectually considered. Appleby found himself feeling differently. Something indefinable in Lord Skillet's bearing, even more than his last slightly crazy remark, made him wonder whether this scion of aristocracy was wholly sane.

'There was also a man called Cave,' he said. 'Cave was the man who came up to the castle with the news that Sutch was dead. But Cave had been in a cave, and mightn't be able to swear that there had been no helicopter. But it is probable that a jury would take my word for it.'

'A jury?' Lord Skillet was all innocent surprise. 'The Coroner's, do you mean?'

'For a start, yes. But another jury may enter the picture later, Lord Skillet. Possibly at the Central Criminal Court. For as the newspapers like to have it, the police are not ruling out the possibility of foul play.'

'Foul play!' Lord Ampersand exclaimed, as if the thought had never occurred to him. 'Do you mean, my dear sir, that somebody may have plotted to *kill* this Sutch fellow? Who on earth would do that?'

'At the moment, I haven't the slightest idea. Perhaps nobody. "Foul play" is a term one can apply rather widely, I suppose.'

'Perhaps,' Lord Skillet asked politely, 'you are turning over in your head my father and myself as likely foul players?'

'Certainly not. I turn nothing over in my head until I have an adequate assemblage of facts there. And that means that there are certain questions I'd like to ask. It will be perfectly proper for you to take exception to my doing so. As you know, I am merely assisting your Chief Constable in an informal way.'

'Man's at least a gentleman,' Lord Ampersand said, turning to his son, and speaking precisely as if he'd forgotten that Appleby was in the room. 'Know where you are with him, eh? Better let him go ahead.'

But at this candid moment there was an interruption, the door of the library opening and a young man coming into the room. He paused, but not as if having been unaware of whom he was going to find there. Then, as it seemed not to occur to either Lord Ampersand or his son to say anything, he addressed himself to Appleby.

'May I introduce myself?' he asked. 'My name is Charles Digitt.'

'And he is going to be my heir,' Lord Skillet said. 'When my poor father passes on, Charles will undoubtedly be my heir. Presumptive, of course. Entirely so until they've ordered my coffin. I imagine Grace and Geraldine will do that. So it's sure to be on the cheap.'

These unseemly remarks didn't discompose young Charles Digitt, who shook hands with Appleby, sat down, and devoted himself to taking stock of the situation.

'Are they all coming out?' he asked presently.

'Are all what coming out, Charles?' It was Lord Ampersand who was perplexed.

'The cats from their bags, Uncle. And scattering in every direction. Some of them getting into cupboards, perhaps, and rattling the family skeletons.'

This, although homelier matter, seemed to be as baffling to Lord Ampersand as the fabled death of Aeschylus had been. Appleby wondered whether it was in some way directed against Lord Skillet. He had detected a glance passing between the two cousins which somehow spoke of a covert war of nerves as existing between them. In an ordinary way first cousins don't much trouble themselves with sibling jealousies. But here there was the special circumstance that the first of them was at one remove and the second of them at two removes from the same marquisate. Appleby, whose more common contacts were with professional persons and a modest gentry, felt unsure of his ground here. He had seen enough in his time of dirty work in the higher reaches of society to form the view that the only fairly constant attribute of the aristocracy consisted in their being rather odd, and in particular in their secretly setting store by distinctions which overtly they made light of. Perhaps this crowd was like that.

But at the moment he'd had a stroke of luck. With the exception of that Miss Deborah Digitt whose existence and possible connection with the hypothetical Ampersand Papers had been revealed by Lady Grace, he'd now had the whole lot on parade. And here at the moment were three male Digitts in a room with him. It wasn't a bad opportunity for beginning to sort things out.

'I don't know about cats in bags,' he said easily, 'but I am, I confess, curious about cupboards. As containing, you know, not skeletons but papers. I have gathered from Lady Grace that Dr Sutch, who has died in so startling and indeed perplexing a fashion, had been employed by you, Lord Ampersand, to search for documents which might prove to be of great interest and equally great financial value. Anybody not assured that Dr Sutch's death was purely accidental would be bound to centre his inquiries on those activities. For example, on the probable legal ownership of anything of the kind that turned up.'

'It isn't plausible,' Charles Digitt said, 'that a man should be murdered—and it seems to be murder that you are talking about, Sir John—over scraps of Shelley and Byron.'

'Not even if they had, potentially, a high sale-room value?'

'Not even then, I'd say—for what my opinion is worth.' Charles now seemed to be speaking quite seriously. 'Literary remains—if that's the term—are not things that people get murdered about. Or not outside harmless fiction.'

'I'm bound to say I agree with my cousin.' Lord Skillet

stretched himself lazily. 'Jewels, yes—or bullion, or even what people stow away in the vaults of a bank. But, somehow, poems and diaries and so forth, not. Murder goes along with glamour. Something of that kind.'

There was a pause which lasted long enough for Appleby to digest the fact that beneath a tiresome frivolity these first cousins were both intelligent men. But he was aware of something else as well. It was as if there were a game of skill in progress and one of the contestants—whether judiciously or not—had exposed an important card upon the table. At least Archie (which he recalled as Lord Skillet's name) and Charles had taken another hard look at one another. And what about Lord Ampersand? During these latter exchanges he would have had to be described as fallen into an abstraction. Perhaps he was merely thinking about his dogs, or about the perplexing fact that nowadays he never seemed to have quite enough money to pay his bills. Or was it about something more germane to the current situation at Treskinnick Castle? Quite unexpectedly, Lord Ampersand now answered this unspoken question in Appleby's mind.

'Tell you an odd thing,' he said to the library at large. 'About that fellow Sutch, you know. Turned uncommonly curious about matters he wasn't being invited to stick his nose into. Did you ever hear'—Lord Ampersand had turned to Appleby—'of the art of war in the Middle Ages?'

'It was quite advanced, no doubt.'

'No, no. It's a book. By a chap called Oboy, or something of the kind.'

'Oman,' Lord Skillet said indulgently. 'But just what are you talking about?'

'Rummaged for it in this very room. And talked about Oliver Cromwell. No connection with Shelley and that lot, at all. I looked them up, you know. And about Treskinnick being reduced. It was damned rum.'

'I suppose,' Archie said, 'that he was going to take advantage of his stay here to write a history of the wretched pile for some antiquarian journal. With profuse acknowledgements to the Most Hon. the Marquess of Ampersand. A spot of kudos. That sort of thing. And some chaps *did* reduce the castle. But, this time, it was the castle, you might say, that reduced Sutch. Such is life, as it were.'

Appleby listened without impatience to this return to frivolity. Let these people exhibit themselves to the full. Even egg them on.

'All sorts of legends,' he offered, 'do attach themselves to a historic place like this. No doubt a siege of Treskinnick is a historical fact, although I know nothing about it. But there must be all sorts of stories of dubious authenticity as well. Sutch may have thought of treating of them too. In lighter vein, one might say.'

'If so, they didn't exactly buoy him up.' Lord Skillet seemed to find this reflection funny. 'But it's all none too relevant, Sir John, to what you appear determined to take in hand.'

'Perfectly true—but it's interesting, all the same. Is there any member of your family who goes in for the annals of the Digitts?'

'Our cousin Deborah.' Charles came out with this decisively, but after a second's pause. 'She lives at Budleigh Salterton, and knows a great deal of family history.'

'Decent woman,' Lord Ampersand said. 'Send her game from time to time. The right thing. Didn't know you saw much of her, Charles.'

'Oh, yes—quite a lot, just recently. Deborah is a delightful woman—lively and cultivated. She owns a great many family papers, too, and could write us up if she wanted to. She's the great-granddaughter of Adrian Digitt, you know. And it's Adrian, in a sense, that we're having all this fuss about.'

'Ah, yes.' Appleby continued mildly interested, 'Would Dr Sutch's researches have taken him at all into Miss Deborah Digitt's company, would you say?'

'I've no idea—no idea, at all. I had very little conversation with poor Sutch. Archie may know. Archie?'

'I've no idea either.' Archie again faintly suggested the poker player. 'We've all wondered from time to time, of course, whether those supposed papers of Adrian Digitt's mayn't be in the old girl's possession, after all. Surely you must have sounded her about that, Charles? If you've really been getting thick with her, that's to say.'

'She's rather close, as a matter of fact, Archie. And your father would be the proper person to inquire.'

It was at this juncture that a violent altercation broke out between certain of Lord Ampersand's dogs in the court-yard outside the library windows, and the conference was thrown into confusion as a result. Appleby took the oppor-tunity to withdraw. He had been given a good deal to think about. Had an officer higher in the hierarchy of the police (only there wasn't one) demanded a statement from him at that moment he would have had to record the im-pression—perhaps the key impression—that a good deal had been going on among the Digitts both before and after the decease of the unfortunate Dr Ambrose Sutch.

XII

LADY AMPERSAND WAS the last person to run to earth. Appleby didn't want to leave Treskinnick Castle without making the acquaintance of its chatelaine. Lady Ampersand, after all, wasn't a Digitt. She might be quite agreeable.

Ludlow, appealed to as he passed through the hall, was confident that there would be no more difficulty in locating her ladyship. It was her jigsaw hour, he explained. This was her invariable pursuit between tea and dressing for dinner, and she invariably prosecuted it in the grey drawing-room. Ludlow made no scruple about immediately conducting Appleby to this apartment. He opened the two leaves of an imposing door, said 'Sir John Appleby' in a loud voice which would have been appropriate to carry over the din of a large party, and withdrew.

Lady Ampersand had for a moment the appearance of greeting her caller with a dramatic gesture ambiguously poised between welcome and arrest. But this was merely because she happened to be holding up in air a small and convoluted fragment of plywood, the better to meditate its place in the puzzle on the table in front of her.

'Ah, yes,' she said. 'How do you do?' Although perhaps reluctant to break off from her absorbing task, she was much too well-bred to be other than graciously welcoming. 'I am so pleased that my daughter Grace thought of you, Sergeant. But when the idea was brought forward I also rang up my sister Agatha, who is a tower of strength when

110

anything disagreeable happens. She was quite clear that you were the person to send for.'

'I'm afraid I'm not a sergeant,' Appleby said. 'I have retired, you see, and am no longer a policeman at all.'

'I don't think it makes any difference. In fact I am sure my husband will be delighted to employ you. And I will see to it that he makes a satisfactory arrangement on the financial side. He is sometimes a little absent-minded in such matters. I think it is going to be the giraffe.'

'I beg your pardon?'

'In the top right-hand corner. The puzzle, you see, is called "Noah's Ark". It arrived from Harrods only this morning.'

'How very interesting.' Appleby advanced to the table. 'Yes, almost certainly the giraffe.' Lady Verinder in *The Moonstone*, he was thinking, was surely the last woman in England to propose the private hire of a detective officer from Scotland Yard. 'Giraffes are creatures readily identifiable by their necks, are they not? But I have always thought their little stumpy horns very characteristic too.'

'So they are.' Lady Ampersand appeared now to have become aware that her visitor was not from the order of society which she had supposed. Her error, however, failed to disturb her. 'Yes,' she said, 'I am so pleased. My husband, you must understand, would be upset if it were discovered that one of us had done something dreadful to that unfortunate man. Not that he wasn't rather tiresome at times. When he wasn't calling Rollo "my lord" he was calling him "your grace". I even distinctly heard him on one occasion say, "May it please your grace". It irritated my husband very much to be mixed up with a duke. Rather a long time ago, it seems, there was an Ampersand who declined a dukedom in exchange for his wife. I have never

111

got to know a great deal about the Digitts. But they appear to have been very odd people at times. Dear me! Here is what must be the trunk of the elephant. Don't you think, Mr . . .?'

'Sir John Appleby. And undoubtedly the trunk. I am sorry to hear that Dr Sutch was so socially insufficient. I wonder whether we might discuss some other aspects of his time at Treskinnick?'

'But certainly, Sir John.' Lady Ampersand took this transition in her stride.

'Can you tell me, for instance, how Lord Ampersand came to get hold of him?'

'He was found somewhere by our son, Archie. It was scarcely a recommendation, to my mind. It would have been better to consult my sister Agatha. Archie, of course, is extremely clever, and my husband relies on him a good deal. But not all of his acquaintance are agreeable, or even presentable.'

'I have no doubt that Lord Skillet possesses catholic tastes, Lady Ampersand. He interested himself, for instance, in this matter of Adrian Digitt's papers?'

'Oh, very much. It was a matter of his feeling there was money in them.'

'Yes, of course. It is only natural. Would his cousin, Mr Charles Digitt, have had the same sort of interest in them?'

'I suppose so. In fact, that is only natural too. Charles will inherit the title, you know, and presumably anything else that there is to inherit. And as the family affairs are somewhat embarrassed, he must be expected to have an eye to anything that might raise the wind.' Lady Ampersand appeared pleased with this free-and-easy expression. 'I am almost sure that here we have the lion's mane. The

112

best puzzles come from Harrods. They have a very special man who knows about them.'

'Reliable tradesmen are a great blessing, are they not? By the way, do you yourself believe that these papers really exist?'

'Certainly I do. In fact, it is my belief that Archie came on them—or on some of them—a long time ago. And I don't think he wanted Dr Sutch about the place one little bit.'

'But didn't you say it was he who found Dr Sutch for the job?'

'Oh, certainly. But it was only because we insisted that a person of that sort should be brought in. He may have thought that Sutch would be less troublesome than anybody else, don't you think? Particularly if he himself had been selling some of those papers in a quiet way already.'

'Dear me, Lady Ampersand! Would your son have been doing that?'

'As a small boy, Sir John, Archie was much given to going to my purse—just as, later, he was given to going to his father's brandy and cigars. As my sister Agatha once said to me, Archie is one of nature's pilferers.' Lady Ampersand paused to fit in the lion's mane. 'It is a weakness, no doubt. But only a small one. I used to feel it distracted his mind from other less trivial failings.'

'It is a reasonable view.' Appleby was conscious that he ought to find all this candour distressing. At the same time he felt a certain respect for Lady Ampersand. Even for her intelligence, in a limited sense. It might almost be said that she knew what she was about. 'Are you saying,' he asked gravely, 'and are you judging it necessary to say, that your son might involve himself in acts of petty dishonesty but would be unlikely to be implicated in major crime?'

113

'That is how my daughter Grace would put it. But then she has always been a plain-spoken girl. A little toad.'

'Your daughter?'

'And, I think, the tail of the second toad. They must all be two by two, of course. Otherwise it would be cheating.'

'Certainly it would.' Appleby felt he had made an unfortunate error. 'But cheating seems to be what we are talking about, Lady Ampersand.'

'So it is. And pilfering. We started from that.'

'Quite so. Would you be inclined to describe it as a kind of hereditary thing among the Digitts? Mr Charles Digitt, for instance. Would he have the same unfortunate instinct to put his hand on things as you say Lord Skillet has?'

'Archie and his cousin Charles don't seem to me to be at all like each other, Sir John. Except that they talk in the same clever way, and often won't stop making fun of people.' Lady Ampersand picked up another fragment of her puzzle, and studied it for an unusual length of time. 'Charles,' she said, as if she had worked something out in her head, 'would always have larger ideas than Archie.'

'A broader point of view, you mean?'

'No, not exactly that.' Lady Ampersand's features now indicated perplexity. She was in deep waters, and knew it. 'Bolder designs,' she said suddenly. 'That's it! How Charles differs from Archie, I mean. And there's something attractive in it, it must be said.'

'A good jigsaw puzzle, for instance, always reveals a bold design?'

'How very true!' Lady Ampersand accorded Appleby a frankly admiring glance. 'And do you know what I think?'

'No, I don't. But I'd like to, very much.'

'I think that in this one there will be some tiny creature so

114

well in the foreground that it will take up quite a lot of space.'.

'I haven't the least doubt you are right. The same effects, as a matter of fact, sometimes occur in detective investigation.'

'Is that so?' Lady Ampersand, although still perplexed, was interested. 'But I have always preferred jigsaws to detective stories. They are more restful, don't you think? And they don't often cheat.'

'Certainly not if they come from Harrods. May I ask you one further question?'

'Please do, Sir John. I am enjoying our little talk very much. It gives me quite a new notion of the police.'

'Ah, yes—the police! Let us consider what we ought to tell my colleagues who are still active in that profession. We are to make it clear to them, are we not, that it would be psychologically quite inept to regard Lord Skillet as one likely to look on the larger, the darker face of crime? Very good. But now, what about your nephew, Charles Digitt? Would you be surprised, for instance, to hear that he had murdered someone? Poor Dr Sutch, say.'

'Oh, very surprised, indeed.' And Lady Ampersand really looked surprised. 'Please tell your subordinates to ignore such an idea entirely. It is out of the question. My daughter Grace says so. And perhaps you should consult my sister Agatha. She would say precisely the same thing.'

'I don't think that will be necessary, Lady Ampersand.' Appleby got to his feet. 'And I am most grateful to you. We are undoubtedly gaining ground.'

'So we are—for here is the rest of the lion.' It was evident that Lady Ampersand's attention had again wandered a little. 'And I do hope you will call again, Sir John. Perhaps you could dine with us one evening quite soon. My husband would be delighted.'

'Thank you very much. It is possible, however, that we shall meet again before that. ' And Appleby glanced at the table. 'The bits and pieces begin to arrange themselves,' he said. 'It's a satisfactory moment when that happens, is it not?'

'Yes, indeed,' Lady Ampersand said.

XIII

JUDITH APPLEBY, CONTACTED on the telephone, was unperturbed by her husband's having to confess to a trick of the old rage. She was used to it. And the Birch-Blackies, it appeared, had mumps in the house and were obliged to scratch their dinner engagement.

'But we have the Ouseleys on Thursday,' Judith said. 'So I hope it will be one of your twenty-four-hour things.'

'What do you mean—my twenty-four-hour things?'

'When you blunder in on some hideous crime early one morning, and sort it all out over the breakfast-table next day.'

'Well, no. It won't be like that. Or not quite like that. For instance, I shall have to pay a call at Budleigh Salterton.'

'At *where*?'

'Budleigh Salterton. And probably bearing a brace of pheasants.'

'Don't be silly. It would be a shocking solecism, and you'd probably be run in as a poacher. Wrong time of year.'

'So it is. A couple of hares, then. With their noses in those little paper bags.'

'Then don't do anything messy with them. Are you in your London suit?'

'Of course I'm not in my London suit. I'm wandering the wilds of Lyonnesse, aren't I? Appropriately clad.'

'And with magic in your eyes. Are you putting up with these lordlings at this Treskinnick place?'

'No, I'm not. That might prove embarrassing, supposing

their affairs to turn out on the murky side. Come to think of it, I wasn't invited, either. I'm at the local pub. It's called the Ampersand Arms.'

'I expect they'll give you a marvellous dinner,' Judith said. 'Or perhaps just what they call a cream tea.' She rang off.

A second telephone call had ensured that Appleby would have somebody with whom to share whatever the inn thought to provide. Inspector Craig arrived before dinner, and while they waited for it they conversed in a corner of the bar.

'Well, sir,' Craig asked cheerfully, 'what did you make of that crowd?'

'That they're *not* a crowd, to start with. We have to deal with a comparatively small *dramatis personae*.'

'Perfectly true—but I suppose a few more characters may yet turn up. And there are some quite choice specimens already. It's hard to believe in Lord Ampersand, for instance.'

'Not as being anything much other than he seems to be, I'd say. And—do you know, Craig?—I'm less hooked on the cast than on the *mise en scène*.'

'Ah, the tower.'

'Just that. By the way, I hear you borrowed a helicopter.'

'Straight away. It simply landed on the roof a chap who then fixed up a rope and pulley affair. I was winched up myself in no time, and I can't say I liked it one little bit. But tomorrow morning we're to have fellows run up a light scaffolding carrying a zigzag of ladders on the inner face of the tower. Not such a job as you'd imagine, it seems. You must honour us, Sir John, by being the first man to make the ascent.' Craig paused to permit himself laughter at this innocent joke. 'Which means I needn't waste your time by describing the muniment room to you now. Nothing all that odd about it—except anyone siting it in such a place. That seems clean barmy to me.'

'Particularly with the staircase as it plainly was. Your helicopter, incidentally, has been putting ideas in Lord Ampersand's head. He thinks that a helicopter came huffing and puffing about the place and blew the blessed staircase down.'

'Well, why not? A helicopter can shatter windows fifty yards away. It could easily . . .'

'You know perfectly well there was no helicopter, Craig.'

'Yes, sir—and perhaps there was no criminal either. Doesn't your mind return to that from time to time? Mine does.'

'Well, yes. But for one simple circumstance, I might settle for that view. A half-rotten structure gives way under a heavy man. Nothing could be more plausible.'

'As, perhaps, it was meant to be.'

'Quite so. But by the one simple circumstance, Inspector, I mean, of course, that rope and cord. There it was, a thoroughly unaccountable thing, and bang on the site of the supposed accident. But as soon as one begins to think in terms of a crime, those unaccountable objects take on an obvious function. Isn't that so?'

'Yes, Sir John. Somebody lies in wait for Sutch at the top of the tower, tips him off the platform, and shins down the rope as it hangs as a loop from the top of the staircase. But the structure doesn't stand up to such treatment, and down it comes too, almost in the instant that the murderer has safely touched ground and bolted.' Craig paused, and shook his head. 'It's the alibi theory we were talking about, more or less. Only it couldn't have happened that way—not *just* that way—for a very sufficient reason that we know.

You happened to be on the spot, Sir John, and you just can't—can you?—square such a sequence of events with your own observations. Not to speak of the rope being left neatly coiled like it was. So none of it makes sense.'

'No more it does—I agree. So try something else, Craig. Why should anybody want to murder this man Sutch, anyway?'

'Sutch had found—up there in that crazy place—a large collection of very valuable papers. He had divulged the fact to somebody with no legal title to their ownership, but who nevertheless proposed to be the sole beneficiary. So he killed Sutch and nobbled the stuff.'

'Nobbled it? Just how?'

'It had already been removed to some hiding-place he'd been told about. He only had to bide his time, and collect.'

'Yes. That *does* make sense, I agree. Or it makes a limited sort of sense in one area of the puzzle. Perhaps we can work outwards from it to a rational view of the whole thing. But there's—well, a piece missing.'

'Or several pieces, sir.' Craig finished his gin-and-french like a man in deepening gloom. 'Do you think,' he asked suddenly, 'that one of them might be that fellow Cave in the cave?'

'Indeed I do. I even believe that Mr Cave may now be hard to lay our hands on. But let's go in to dinner.'

So Sir John Appleby and Inspector Craig went in to dinner. It was to find that another guest had established himself at table before them. And that this guest was the missing Mr Cave.

XIV

IF SIR JOHN Appleby was startled at having a prediction suddenly negatived, Mr Cave—that devoted speleologist—appeared to be startled too. For a moment, indeed, he looked at the new arrivals with eyes wide open in alarm. Then, rather oddly, he could be observed to take the deep breath of a man from whom some doubt or indecision has been removed. At the same time, he was sufficiently confused to half-rise from his chair and at once sit down again.

'Oh, good-evening!' he said. 'Sir John Appleby, of course.'

'Good-evening. I am delighted to meet you again so soon. Let me introduce Inspector Craig, of the County Constabulary. The Inspector may be said to be tidying up that unfortunate affair at the castle. Inspector, this is Mr Cave.'

'How do you do, sir?' If Craig was astonished, he didn't show it. 'Sir John and I were recently having a word about you, as a matter of fact. We're not without the thought that you may be of help to us. Assist the police in their inquiries, as the newspapers say.'

'Oh, yes—yes, of course.' Mr Cave spoke jerkily. 'Shall we—well, dine together? This table is laid that way.'

Before this proposition Inspector Craig discernibly hesitated, as if feeling some impropriety in thus breaking bread with one on whom he might presently be clapping a pair of handcuffs. Appleby, however, made no bones about it, and set the example of sitting down at once.

'Capital!' he said. 'We can share a bottle of wine—supposing the place runs to anything tolerable in that way. As you and Dr Sutch perhaps did, Mr Cave, when you had that interesting chat with him not very long ago.'

'Yes, indeed, yes. It has been extremely sad. And worrying.'

'Ah, worrying. Perhaps it has been worrying that has brought you back here? It has been our impression, you know, that you were glad to make your escape from the district.'

'My escape, Sir John? I hardly . . .'

'To place yourself at some remove, shall we say, from so distressing an episode. I see that this rather grubby bill of fare speaks of fillet steak. Shall we risk it? We could hedge the bet a little by asking them to make it the basis of a mixed grill.' Appleby picked up another card. 'I'd be more inclined to have the so-called *Bordeaux rouge* rather than venture among châteaux with wholly mysterious names.'

'Yes, I agree—I quite agree.' Cave was clearly grateful for this breathing-space. 'I have came back to Treskinnick,' he went on abruptly, 'with some thought of contacting the police. Yes, that has been it. So this has really been a fortunate meeting. It enables me, so to speak, to take the bull by the horns. But it may be that a glass of wine . . .'

The wine was fetched. The mixed grill was quite briskly put in hand, as certain smells and sizzlings through a hatch in the wall testified. Mr Cave nervously crumbled a roll of some antiquity on his plate. He took a gulp of wine.

'I want to confess,' he said abruptly.

Inspector Craig, distinctly alarmed, fumbled indecisively for a notebook. He was having a vision, no doubt, of counsel for the defence making devastating play with the irregularity of the occasion. But Appleby, although looking grave, again didn't stand upon the forms.

'That you have so far,' he asked, 'not been quite so communicative as you might have been on circumstances known to you which could have some bearing on the manner of Dr Sutch's death?'

'Just that. If I may say so, Sir John, you phrase it very well. Dr Sutch and I were—well, meditating what might be called a partnership.'

'Does that mean, Mr Cave'—it was Craig who came in grimly with this—'that you and Dr Sutch were fabricating some sort of plot together?'

'Well, yes. I suppose it might be expressed that way. But it came to nothing, you see. It came to nothing at all.'

'May we pause,' Appleby asked, 'at this point? And may I say a word, Mr Cave, about the law of conspiracy? It is complex and tricky—and, in fact, worries jurists a good deal. Suppose you sit down alone in a room, and draw up on paper a detailed plan for committing some atrocious crime. And suppose that paper to fall into the hands of Inspector Craig. He cannot, on the mere strength of it, charge you with any indictable offence. You might think you were in a position analogous to that of a man found loitering with intent to commit a felony. But—if I understand the matter aright—it just doesn't work that way. You have merely been amusing yourself, it can be held, by concocting a piece of crime-fiction such as may be bought at any bookstall. But suppose you had a companion in that room, and that you went at your concoction together. The circumstances might, of course, be such that there was nothing in question except a harmless literary collaboration. Nevertheless the shadow of conspiracy—a very tricky thing, as I say—might be hanging over you. And if you are found to have conspired to commit a crime you won't be much assisted by the fact that you never got round to it. It is an area of the law surrounded, I admit, by every sort of dubiety. But, roughly speaking, that's it.'

This long speech was perhaps not the less effective as being delivered in no sort of intimidatory manner. It was evident that the mixed grill, which had now arrived, was going to present Cave with considerable problems in the way of mastication. Presumably his mouth had gone dry, since he took two swigs at his wine in rapid succession. It looked, indeed, as if another bottle might be required before this conference was concluded. (And Craig's hypothetical barrister would certainly inquire about that.) 'Sutch and I,' Cave said with an effort, 'turned out, you see, to have certain interests in common. We were both on the track of the *Nuestra Señora del Rosario*.'

'Of the *what*?' Craig demanded.

'Not the flagship of 1588, of course. That had to surrender, as you know.' Cave had suddenly the manner of an earnestly informative professor addressing his pupils. 'A much later galleon of the same name. In fact it was taking specie and bullion to Ireland.'

'And, no doubt, was wrecked near Treskinnick,' Appleby said. He was conscious that this new and improbable dimension of the Ampersand affair wasn't quite so new, after all. In some dim way, it had already glimmered in his head. Had it been when Lord Skillet said something idle about what people get themselves killed on account of, and what they don't? He couldn't remember. But at least he was prepared to listen to Mr Cave with an open mind.

Inspector Craig was not so disposed. He had even produced what might be called an angry snort.

'That kind of yarn again!' he said. 'Scores of them drifting around these parts—and a damned nuisance they are every time. People out on the beaches and among the rocks with their metal-detectors, thinking they're going to turn up the iron-work on ancient chests and then sure to find no end of gold coins inside. Fighting one another for their pitches, even, like fossickers in yarns of the Wild West. Not to speak of those that go skin-diving and get themselves drowned—and better men drowned too, from time to time.'

'No doubt,' Appleby said—and refrained from any hinted reproof of this outburst. 'But the death we have on our hands now wasn't by water. Mr Cave, surely Dr Sutch's interests were quite remote from Spanish treasure, and that sort of thing? I don't know about your own.'

'Sutch had got up the whole history of Treskinnick Castle and the Digitts, and had come upon something that looked rather more than a legend. At some date early in the seventeenth century just such a treasure was discovered by a member of the family. It had been buried in sand, or washed into a cave, several decades earlier. The then earl decided to hang on to it quietly for a time, because he feared the interposition of the Crown, should he announce the find. That makes sense, wouldn't you say, Sir John?'

'Yes, it does. Sense so far.'

'Then came the Civil War, and the stories differ. According to one, the entire treasure was disbursed in the royalist cause. According to another, it was simply hidden away yet more securely—so securely that it escaped discovery when the castle was captured. And more than that. So securely, that its whereabouts perished out of mind.'

'And the very memory of it?' Appleby asked sharply. 'This was something Sutch discovered that the present Digitts didn't know?'

'Not quite that, I imagine, Sir John. Rather, perhaps,

something that they had long ago fallen into the habit of not believing in.'

'It wouldn't be possible that Sutch had been brought to Treskinnick, whether by one member of the family or another, ostensibly to examine family papers but actually to run this supposed treasure to earth?'

'No, I don't think so.' Cave looked slightly bewildered. 'In fact, I am sure not. Or at least Dr Sutch would have been being extremely disingenuous with me, were it so.'

'Whereas,' Craig demanded, 'you were in fact being completely candid with one another. We've heard the story he told you. May we now have the story you told him?'

'Yes, indeed.' Cave nodded nervously. 'For a number of years I have made a study of all the records of foundered galleons and the like. And also of the activities of wreckers and smugglers: all that sort of thing. Particularly in relation to natural hiding-places along the coast.'

'And that,' Appleby asked, 'is why you go poking round all those caverns and grottoes and pot-holes and so on?'

'Well, yes.'

'It has been less a scientific interest than a matter of possible gain?'

'Both, Sir John. I assure you—distinctly both.'

'No doubt. And so we come to Treskinnick. You and Sutch meet, and begin cautiously to explore one another's minds. And then you decide to join forces. Would that be right?'

'Perfectly right. He had this specific information about the *Nuestra Señora del Rosario*. And I had my special knowledge of caves and so on as hiding-places.'

'You were simply proposing to find this treasure and quietly make off with it?'

'Something like that. Yes, I am afraid so.'

'And it is merely this intention that perturbs you now that Sutch has died in mysterious circumstances, and that you have judged it prudent to make what you call a "confession" of? Or does the story continue?'

'Continue, Sir John? I fear I don't understand you.'

'There has been a plan, or plot. Well, did anything come of it? Did you and Sutch continue in what may be termed amity, or did you by any chance fall out between yourselves? And did you discover anything? For example, that cave from which I saw you emerge some seconds—or was it minutes?—after Sutch's death: just where and how far does it go? Right under the castle, I suppose. Can there be any question of there having been, or even being now, a passage connecting it with the upper reaches of the North Tower?'

Not unnaturally, this rain of questions had an unnerving effect upon the eminent speleologist. Then a further recourse to his glass a little rallied him.

'No, no,' he said. 'We certainly didn't quarrel, Sutch and myself. There was no occasion for such a thing, since we were neither of us really any nearer what we were after. At least I wasn't. But I am bound to say that Sutch was irritatingly reticent at one point. He had been very thorough in searching and sounding the castle for possible hiding-places, but with no success. He told me all about that. But then, one day, he said he had a theory, all the same. He wouldn't say more than that. Except that it had been put in his head by an architect. I was a little put out by his failing to be quite frank with me. Frankness had been in our bargain, you know.' Cave hesitated. 'And it may have cost him his life, if you ask me.'

'And just what do you mean by that, Mr Cave?'

It was Craig who had asked this question—and quite

127

without Sir John Appleby's urbanity. And Cave, as a consequence, was at once extremely upset.

'I don't mean anything at all!' he cried. 'I mean that what I mean is . . .' He took another gulp of wine.

'At least you seem to be accepting the view that Sutch was murdered—presumably by somebody with whom he was now sharing a secret?'

'Nothing of the kind!' Cave seemed now to be casting about in his mind in mere panic. 'I know nothing about how Sutch died. It is entirely mysterious to me. I was thinking merely that, if he had divulged his theory to me, we might together have hit upon the treasure at once. And then he wouldn't have been on that staircase when he *was* on it. So he wouldn't have fallen with it when it fell.'

'I see.' It was Appleby who spoke again now—and mildly. 'And that is really all you have to tell us, Mr Cave?'

'Oh, yes. Absolutely. I don't know anything more—anything more at all.'

'Then we are obliged to you for what you have been able to tell us.' Appleby put down his table-napkin. 'And I think we can cut out the biscuits and cheese.'

XV

IT WAS NOON on the following day before Appleby
returned to Treskinnick Castle. He had spent the earlier
part of the morning on a fairly long walk: a cliff walk for the
most part, but by the seashore when it was possible to get
down to it. It was still a surprisingly empty coast. Here and
there a hamlet—it might be no more than three or four
fishermen's cottages—nestled at the foot of creek or cove,
but there were hardly any other habitations visible. Whatever was around had been around for a long time. Caravan
parks such as erupt and proliferate like uncomfortable
cutaneous diseases in most maritime regions of England
were for some reason entirely absent. It was possible, in
fact, to think of a great deal of the scene as totally undisturbed between the ages of the first Elizabeth and the
second. There was food for thought in this. Just what,
conceivably, thus lay undisturbed in Lord Ampersand's
stately if dilapidated home? Those literary remains of
Adrian Digitt which connected him with the great figures
of the Romantic Revival? That was to think in terms only
of the day before yesterday, but at least it wasn't wholly
improbable. Doubloons and pistoles bearing the image of
Philip II of Spain? Perhaps that might be called at once a
more commonplace and a less likely conjecture.

And was either of them really mixed up with the death of
Dr Ambrose Sutch? Either of them *might* be. Indeed, their
existence or postulated existence—whether pistoles or
papers—seemed a little to increase the probability that

129

Sutch's death had not been an accidental one. The hunt for valuable objects that have long lain concealed provides a plausible sort of context or occasion for a criminal act. But, as with Oranges or Lemons, there appeared to be a choice that had to be made. If sheer mischance hadn't been the death of Sutch, then *either* the Ampersand Papers *or* the Ampersand Spanish gold had been. These disparate things surely defied any lumping together as constituting a single motive or main-spring in the case. Or did they? Common sense seemed to say that it must be so. But logic? Logic, Appleby saw, had, so far, nothing to say about the matter at all. There were still too many missing pieces in the Sutch affair to permit of any confident intellectual dealing with it. Appleby was not yet out of the twilight world of intuitions and hunches—and hadn't he warned Inspector Craig that hunches were chancy things? Nevertheless, one hunch he'd indulge himself in. Both Lord Skillet and his cousin Charles Digitt were at the heart of the mystery—or poised, say, at an equal distance from that heart. The image was that of a seesaw. Or was it rather that of two duellists, eyeing one another each at an equal number of paces from the dropped handkerchief? And then what about Cave, that far from disinterested speleologist? Could any hunch yank him into the cloudy picture—or at least further into it than his own confession had taken him? There is nothing truer about thieves than that they fall out—so mightn't Cave and Sutch have found themselves in a lethal confrontation—a duel deadlier than whatever was the duel that Archie and Charles were engaged in?

Useless rhetorical questions, Appleby told himself—and turned round to make his way back to Treskinnick.

The scaffolding was up: a light tubular structure, apparently niched into the wall of the tower, and supporting, as

Craig had foretold, a criss-cross of fairly short ladders. There was nothing intimidating about it, and nobody stood guard over it. Craig's men had perhaps decided that all they needed to know about the muniment room they already knew. Appleby scarcely supposed that their confidence would be misplaced. Nevertheless it was possible that he himself might have some luck as a snapper-up of one or another unconsidered trifle. He made the ascent briskly, but paused once or twice to glance below him. Since the foot of each ladder rested on solid planking, it would have been difficult so to tumble as to risk more than the breaking of a limb. This didn't mean that looking down at the inner ward would be agreeable if one had no head for heights. The original wooden staircase, turning an angle, as it had done, to ascend the face of the tower virtually overhanging the sea, must have been an even nastier affair. He was astonished that it should ever have been contrived, and more astonished at the bizarre behaviour of the present generation of Digitts in having brought it into requisition again. As for the inner ward, it was a secluded kind of place, surrounded in the main by blank walls. If one had wanted to come and go to the so-called muniment room unobtrusively, it wouldn't have been hard to do so. How much of that had there been, before Sutch and the staircase had gone to their ruin together? It was again an idle question.

But there did seem to be one certainty. Between the moment of that catastrophe and the arrival of the forces of the law in their borrowed helicopter any conceivable activity in the muniment room had been suspended. The original spiral staircase was presumably as impassably choked up as ever. It must, indeed, be in total ruin. Otherwise the bird-watching Lord Ampersand would surely have contrived to bring it into use again. Mediaeval castles, of course, are popularly supposed to be replete with secret passages and staircases—not to speak of concealed dungeons and much else. But the simple structure of this grim tower rendered anything of the sort extremely unlikely.

As Appleby climbed higher his situation became increasingly blowy. Down in the inner ward there had been no effect of wind at all, but it was different up here. One could even tell oneself that a small gale was blowing; that it was chasing itself round and round the tower with the speed of a kitten in pursuit of its own tail. The final ladder didn't exactly wobble but it did rather uncomfortably quiver. It ended on a small platform outside what had apparently been a glazed window. The window had been removed and a stiff tarpaulin hung in its place—as a protection, it was to be supposed, against any sudden worsening of the elements. Appleby was quite glad to have finished his little climb.

The tarpaulin stirred as he confronted it, and was then drawn back with an oddly ceremonious effect which was increased by what was revealed. Ludlow stood within, holding the thing back to afford Appleby entrance, and actually making a composed and formal bow. He might have been going to announce that Lord Ampersand was, or was not, at home.

'Good-morning, Sir John,' Ludlow said. 'Please come in. Mind the step.'

Appleby minded the step—as he had been rather carefully doing during the past five minutes. There was considerable relief in standing on a flagged stone floor.

'Good-morning, Mr Ludlow.' Appleby glanced round the large, much cluttered, room, and saw that the butler was not alone. There was a workman in a far corner of it, seemingly engaged in gathering up and stowing away in a canvas bag a miscellaneous collection of tools. He probably accounted for Ludlow's somewhat surprising presence. The butler judged that this person ought not to be left unattended amid the ancestral proliferations concentrated in the place. 'They've made quick work with those ladders,' Appleby said.

'Yes, indeed, sir. They were on the job at dawn, pretty well, and finished and gone in no time. But the police left only half an hour ago. Taking photographs and the like, they were—all with his lordship's permission, of course. Some of them are to be back later, it seems, and I'm here until that happens.'

'Very proper, I'm sure.'

'I've been doing a little clearing-up meanwhile. I wouldn't think to send any of the under-servants up those things. It's different if you've been in the navy.'

'Ah, yes—of course.' Appleby glanced curiously at this very upper upper-servant, who seemed a little anxious to explain himself. 'And the navy lent a hand at the start, I gather.'

'And a very neat operation it was, Sir John. But they only had to drop a rating or two on the flat roof, you know. There's a trap door giving access from that, as you can see.'

'Quite so.' Appleby directed his gaze upwards and verified this statement. 'It's a curious set-up, Mr Ludlow. Really very curious, indeed. Did the unfortunate Dr Sutch quite take to it?'

'He seemed to, all right.'

'Perhaps at one time he was in the navy too.'

'I'd judge not, Sir John.' Ludlow responded to this perhaps frivolous suggestion with some severity. 'Never out of libraries and the like in his life, if you ask me.'

'Well, his last occupation wasn't exactly a sheltered one.'

Appleby paused on this. 'Mr Ludlow, do you recall saying something to me about a key?'

'A key, Sir John?'

'The key of this muniment room. To the door over there, I suppose, that let one in from the top of the wooden staircase.'

'Quite correct, sir. It was hung up just outside my pantry. And kept coming and going. That's what I said, I think.'

'It certainly was. And you spoke of people coming and going as well. A general effect of there being something a little odd in the way of activity up here. I suppose you have communicated those thoughts of yours to Inspector Craig?'

'Yes, I have—although not too willingly, if you understand me. In my position, I have to consider myself as in a relationship of confidence with the family. If I knew about what you might call mere goings on, it would be no business of mine to divulge them. But the situation changes, I can see, when people start breaking their necks.'

'A very proper point of view. And you and I needn't talk more about these things now.'

'Much better not, I'd say.' Ludlow had directed a disapproving look at the workman, presumably a kind of rearguard to the scaffolding gang, who was showing signs of interest in what he could catch of this conversation. The death of Dr Sutch, after all, must have been sensational news throughout this entire region. Ludlow turned to the workman. 'Now then,' he said. 'About finished, are you?' He might have been a petty officer briskening up just such a rating as he had recently been speaking of.

'Take it easy, pal.' The workman had no disposition to regard himself as under discipline. 'You're not on a bloody quarter-deck, you know, and never were. A menial, that's what you are. A bleeding lackey of the idle rich. But I'm off, all right.' He picked up and shouldered his heavy bag of tools. 'Sweating it out and risking our own flipping necks, we've been, while you've been taking round the early-morning tea to a lot of parasites. Drop dead, and I'd die of laughing.'

'That will do, my man.' Ludlow spoke with proper *hauteur* in face of this atrociously offensive and subversive harangue. 'You may go.'

The workman went. Or, rather, he had reached the window now serving as a door, when Appleby spoke.

'One moment,' Appleby said mildly. 'You haven't got quite all your gear, I think.' And he pointed to a corner of the room where, almost concealed behind a litter of papers, lay what appeared to be a heavy mallet and chisel. The workman walked over to them.

'Not ours,' he said briefly.

'Are you sure? They look just the sort of thing for getting your scaffolding wedged into the wall.'

'Nothing to do with us, mate.' The workman glanced at Appleby indifferently, offered the ghost of a rude gesture to Ludlow, walked back to the window, and disappeared.

'Quite shocking,' Ludlow said. 'He ought to be reported. But what would that do? A word from his employer, and the whole lot would be "out", as they call it, and living fat on Social Security. I'd give them Social Security with a stick, I would, if I had my way. And when working, mark you, for one of the principal noblemen in the Duchy! A regular disgrace.'

'Ah, well!' Appleby said. 'If I had to be scrambling about all day like a monkey on a stick, Mr Ludlow, I dare say I'd enjoy giving a bit of lip from time to time. We must be tolerant when dealing with the simpler classes of society. I suppose you wouldn't know anything about that mallet and chisel?'

'Nothing at all. Except that I'd have expected one of those blundering policeman to notice it and ask about it.'

'So should I, I'm afraid—except that every manner of rubbish appears to have been dumped here at one time or another. The things couldn't have been brought in since the police left, could they?'

'Certainly they could not—unless that impudent fellow was lying. Or, of course, unless I am.'

'Quite so.' Appleby was now prowling round the muniment room, his eyes on the flagstones beneath his feet. 'Mr Ludlow, when Dr Sutch was doing that tapping and measuring and so on in the castle did he ever actually get round to attacking the fabric with tools like these?'

'Certainly not, Sir John. He'd have heard of it if he had.'

'And have *been* heard. It's not a thing you could do without people being aware of it. By the way, I have a notion Inspector Craig told me that Mr Charles Digitt is an architect. Would that be right?'

'Quite right, sir. Mr Charles has to have a profession, I suppose, being a bit out and away from the title at present. Converts things, I've been told.'

'Converts them?'

'Mucking around with pig-sties so that they look like gentrified cottages. All that.'

'Ah, I understand. But now listen to this, Mr Ludlow. I have had it from one witness—perhaps not a particularly reliable one—that Dr Sutch was searching for something quite other than family papers . . .'

'I'd believe him as to that.' Ludlow was surprisingly emphatic. 'That Sutch was after something deep, if you ask me.'

'Quite so—and the question may be exactly *how* deep. But Sutch—so this witness told me—had a theory, and it was a theory that Sutch said had been put in his head by an architect. Can you make anything of that?'

'Something about the way castles were built in the olden time. That would be my guess.'

'And a very good one, I'd be inclined to say, Mr Ludlow. Perhaps Mr Digitt made some suggestion to Dr Sutch.'

'You could ask him, couldn't you?' Quite unexpectedly, Ludlow's features assumed a humorous cast. 'Mr Charles, that is. Not Sutch.'

'I must make a note of it. By the way, where did one get into this chamber from the original spiral staircase?'

'On the other side from this, Sir John. To the left, behind those stuffed animals.'

'It's a regular zoo, isn't it? Can one peer down the thing?'

'Not now, sir. The entrance has been bricked up.'

'I see. And long ago, I suppose.'

'No time ago, at all. I remember when you could open a door, and there below you was this great mass of broken stone. There was a bombardment, you know, and the castle took a great hammering, in the time of the Cavaliers and Roundheads. You'll have heard of them. But when this was made into a muniment room—lumber-room would be more like, if you ask me—they thought it a dusty sort of thing, particularly when the gales blew. So they walled it up.'

'Very sensible. What about the other end of the old staircase?'

'Just the same, Sir John. Or, rather, it's clear as far as the first storey, and after that all collapsed and jam-packed again. I don't reckon a rat could get up it.'

'Ah, that's a pity. It can't have been a rat that startled Dr

Sutch and sent him tumbling. Or scores of rats that went gnawing at the wooden staircase until it collapsed with the poor man. Another hypothesis negatived. But we have to work by elimination, you know.'

'So I've been told, Sir John.' Ludlow, although not appearing to resent this levity, moved to the window. 'Perhaps you'd be thinking,' he asked, 'of looking round at your leisure? I could leave you to it, and the police sergeant will be back quite soon.'

'Yes, by all means, Mr Ludlow. I'm afraid I've already taken up too much of your time.'

'Not at all. It has been a privilege to discuss matters with one of your authority, Sir John.'

And with this courteous speech Lord Ampersand's butler withdrew through the window and slowly sank out of sight—like some supernatural personage on a stage, Appleby thought, being winched through a trap into the nether regions.

XVI

LEFT TO HIS own devices, Appleby decided to begin his
exploration by climbing higher still. There was an old
ladder that could be perched against the trap-door in the
roof. He sited it, mounted to the top, and managed with
some heave and shove to get a heavy wooden cover dis-
placed and himself out on the leads. Although he was
almost in the centre of the large space, and therefore many
yards from the crenellated verge of the tower, it was with a
certain caution that he got to his feet. He may have felt that
the wind might be so robust up here that it could take him
like a leaf and blow him into what was coming to be known
as the Celtic Sea. *And oh ye dolphins waft the hapless youth.* But
he wasn't a youth and he wasn't going to be hapless—or not
here and now. He walked across the broad and barely
sloping roof, leant over the battlements where they came
breast-high, and admired the view. It was worth admiring.
Sea and land were alike in bright sunshine. Moors and
mountains lay available for inspection to the south. To the
west one could imagine oneself looking past the tip of
Ireland for the purpose of taking a glance at Nova Scotia.

After a few minutes, however, and by dint of hazardously
leaning over and boldly peering down, Appleby took a good
look at Treskinnick Castle and its immediate environs
themselves. From up here, he supposed, some resolute
Digitt—an earl, perhaps, though not yet a marquess—had
surveyed the advancing forces of the men who were to
turn England into a commonwealth, and had no doubt

commanded the hanging out of sundry defiant banners on his walls. But the day of banners had been really over, and these disagreeable great squires and great merchants had deployed their cannon and let fly. There must be history books describing how much damage had been done. Sieges and capitulations at just that period, Appleby vaguely supposed, had sometimes been rather formal and ritualized affairs. You surrendered your castle in a dignified way when the water, or perhaps just the claret, ran out. At other times these occasions had been bloody enough, and extremely destructive. How it had been at Treskinnick, he had no idea. It was a subject which Dr Sutch would certainly have got up.

Appleby climbed down into the muniment room again, still thinking about Lord Ampersand's late lamented archivist. He recorded to himself the impression that Dr Sutch must have been an orderly character. At least half the available space was crammed with junk—with the stuffed animals preponderating. These creatures huddled together, nose to tail and haunch to haunch, as if some perfectly appalling danger were constraining them to a quite unnatural contiguity. The majority were in very poor condition, either bursting through their skins or shrinking within their skeletons. Several had shed tails and one or two were short of an eye, so that the general effect was of some fiendish act of cruelty being perpetrated against an unoffending lower creation. But even upon this huddle of decayed taxidermy there appeared to have been a recent attempt at imposing a certain orderliness. Some of the creatures had been shunted round—and were even ranged two by two, as in Lady Ampersand's jigsaw. Perhaps this had been the work of the police, but Appleby rather supposed that Sutch had had a hand in it. Certainly there were evidences that he had been a systematic worker. The papers dispersed in mere piles and bundles here and there had been so discarded because quite evidently of no significance: they fell within the general category of obsolete sales-catalogues and telephone directories. On two long tables and a range of open shelves everything was as neat as could be. And this would probably prove true of the contents of a couple of steel filing-cabinets were a key available to open them.

Appleby sat down on an upturned dinghy (surely a quite crazy thing to lug up to such a place) and tentatively turned his mind to the subject of Adrian Digitt and his remains. It was worth remarking, he told himself, how readily Adrian withdrew, as it were, into a background whenever there sailed into view that highly improbable craft, the second *Nuestra Señora del Rosario*. Even the minds of retired Police Commissioners harbour pockets of juvenile fancy. And one had known all about buried treasure and pirate hoards (*Pieces of Eight! Pieces of Eight!*) long before one had heard of Shelley and what Lord Ampersand would call that crowd. Still, this affair began with the real or supposed Ampersand Papers. There could be no doubt of that.

So start there. There was the extraordinary fact that the wholesale transfer of every sort of paper and document in the castle to this unlikely repository had followed upon, and been the consequence of, a learned world beginning to take some interest in Adrian Digitt. Essentially this bore the appearance of a freakish joke and nothing else. But was it not an improbably laborious joke as well? Suppose that somebody—and presumably some member of the family—had come upon some scattered papers of interest and value, and suppose it were in this person's interest both to discourage qualified scholarly investigation and to secure conditions under which he could himself go to work at leisure in the interest of discovering further treasures of this entirely literary order. Might not that person . . .?

There was no point in dotting the *i*'s and crossing the *t*'s here, Appleby reflected. On evidence, or at least suggestion, already available to him, all this pointed straight at Lord Skillet, whose own mother believed that he had been in some pilfering relationship to Adrian's papers for some time back. Suppose that, this being the situation, Sutch had been more or less wished on Lord Skillet, but had been at the same time Lord Skillet's accomplice or creature. And suppose that Sutch had then made a really major find. Here, again, it might have been a matter of thieves falling out—not over specie, but over diaries and letters and poems and the lord knew what. Sutch might have taken fright, wanted to turn honest, proposed to dump the lot on Lord Ampersand. Whereupon Lord Skillet (by means at present scarcely obvious) might have brought about his demise.

If this were the general picture, where was the main body of Adrian's remains now? Where had they been at the time of Sutch's death? If here in the muniment room, it would be necessary to believe that they were here in the muniment room still. But that was improbable. The booty over which Sutch and Lord Skillet were falling out would already have been removed elsewhere by mutual agreement—with the consequence that, upon Sutch's death, they were within Lord Skillet's sole control. At this point Appleby found himself wishing heartily that he could persuade himself that Sutch's death had been indeed an accident; had simply happened to happen, as it were, while this intrigue was going on. For, if only this were so, Appleby could very happily rid himself of the whole affair. Digitts pinching things from one another need be no concern of his.

No doubt it was his duty as a citizen to unmask petty crime if he came across it. But he'd done a great deal of his duty in his time. Were the wrong Digitt to cash in on Adrian's remains, Appleby—very scandalously, no doubt—would find his sleep quite undisturbed by a knowledge of the fact. Murder, unfortunately, was another matter.

So carry on—and approach the thing from another angle: that of Charles Digitt. Where, in the set-up Appleby had just been imagining, did that young man come in? For he *did* come in: Appleby felt assured of that. Perhaps he had simply tumbled to what his cousin and Sutch were up to between them, and had been demanding his share of the loot. Appleby didn't think very much of this simple theory, which left too many aspects of Charles Digitt—even if aspects only insecurely sensed—out in the cold. The Spanish gold beckoned again here. Sutch (if the wretched Cave was to be believed) had formed a theory about that. And the theory had been put in his head by an architect—who might well have been Charles Digitt.

Appleby heaved himself off the dinghy and fell to pacing the muniment room. What this thought tied up with was obviously the business of Sutch prowling through the castle, tapping and sounding for hiding-places. Surely what he had picked up from Charles—*and from Charles in his character as an architect*—was a particularly likely place in which to look, whether for bullion or for Adrian Digitt's papers.

As he arrived at this not very recondite hypothesis, Appleby chanced to let his eye fall on that mallet and chisel which the young workman had disclaimed, and the use and provenance of which he had discussed with Ludlow. They were eminently instruments, he again reflected, for breaking through substantial barriers of stone. Ludlow had been confident that in the castle itself Sutch could not have so employed them without detection. *But what about up here?* The sudden obviousness of this question almost took Appleby aback.

He picked up the tools and examined them carefully. Each gave off a fine grey powder as he gently brushed it with a finger, and he took this as an indication that they had been quite recently in use. But where, and for what purpose? It was scarcely possible to suppose that Adrian Digitt's papers had ever actually been immured behind or beneath stone and mortar. But a treasure in the unmetaphorical sense of precious metals, coins, plate, jewels was quite a different matter. If you had possessed yourself of such a thing with no secure legal entitlement to it, and if this was a fact rumoured among your enemies, some such operation was likely enough. So the *Nuestra Señora del Rosario* was making the running again.

The most obvious place of concealment of such a kind up here was behind the bricked-up doorway which had originally given upon the spiral staircase. But obvious hiding-places are scarcely good ones. And moreover Ludlow had declared that he recollected a time when you could still open the door there and come on nothing but the broken stone left after the collapse of the staircase, which had presumably taken place during the siege. Where else could one think of? 'Beneath the floor' would be another fairly obvious answer. Already, indeed, and in the obscurely intuitive way in which his mind sometimes worked, Appleby had found himself casting a considering eye over the flagstones with which the entire muniment room was paved. But what lay beneath them? Ultimately, it was a further chamber, and one to which access was no longer possible. But on what sort of structure would the formidable weight of stone now beneath his feet be supported? Here at least was a question for an architect. Appleby was inclined to guess that some sort of fairly shallow stone vaulting must be involved. And this might conceivably mean that at each corner of the structure there would be hollow spaces—perhaps filled with rubble which could be readily removed, and thus freed to accommodate bags or small chests or the like.

All this speculation seemed extremely absurd; seemed, indeed, of a wholly juvenile order. As he set himself to scrutinize the floor virtually inch by inch, Appleby was rather glad that none of Inspector Craig's men had as yet turned up again. The process of inspection was laborious and slow, since every sort of junk had to be moved around as he worked. And the final result was wholly negative. Nowhere over a substantial area in each of the four corners of the muniment room was there the slightest indication of a flagstone having been tampered with. But this, of course, didn't quite conclude matters. Even beneath the central part of floor there might be the effect of at least a shallow cavity, in which it would have been possible to spread out thousands and thousands of pieces of eight.

To test this possibility it looked as if he would have to operate upon what he had come to think of as the Ampersand Zoo in a big way. The creatures extended to the middle of the room, and at its centre to a little beyond that. Appleby began boldly with what came first to hand: a really handsome but unfortunately particularly mouldy stag standing upon a sort of low pedestal vaguely representing rock and heather. Had this pedestal lately been moved already? Faint lines in the dust surrounding it suggested that this might be so. With considerable effort, Appleby shifted the position of the stag's nearest neighbours, and then the stag itself. And his pertinacity

was at once rewarded in the most startling fashion.
A neat circular hole had been hewn in the stone, of a size
adequate to admit a hand and arm. It must have been a
laborious job—so decidedly so that for a moment Appleby
judged that it simply didn't make sense. Wouldn't it have
been much easier to prize up the entire flagstone in which it
had been cut? But that, it immediately came to him, might
well have been beyond a single man's strength. And from
this came the inference that it was a lone operator that had
been involved in this curious performance. It seemed most
improbable that he could have been other than the late Dr
Ambrose Sutch.

The mysterious aperture was perhaps no more than a
foot from the dead centre of the muniment room. Had it
been near an outer wall, one might have conjectured—in
such mediaeval surroundings—that nothing more than
some primitive form of sanitation was involved. But of
course nothing of that kind was in question. Here was the
point at which any system of vaulting that lay below would
make its nearest approach to the floor on which Appleby
now stood. This small chasm had been contrived in order to
render possible some inspection of the inaccessibly sealed-
off chamber below. So it was very simple, indeed. Some of
Inspector Craig's men, he told himself grimly, deserved a
bad mark. They ought as a matter of routine to have
scanned every inch of the place—shoved around the whole
zoo and everything else. It wouldn't be for him, however, to
point this out. With Craig, indeed, it was going to be quite
awkward to be sufficiently casual about what it had been
left to a peripatetic retired policeman to discover.

Dr Sutch had certainly not chipped so pertinaciously
away in the interest of tracking down Adrian Digitt's
remains. What had come to be believed about the history of

the North Tower was quite clear. It had taken such a battering from the engines of Oliver Cromwell more than 300 years ago that its staircase had been demolished and its upper ranges rendered inaccessible ever since—except, indeed, by the hazardous external structure that the bird-watching Lord Ampersand had caused to be erected.

It was evident that all this had been implicitly believed. Yet it became nonsense as soon as one took a hard look at it. It would be nonsense, for instance, to an architect giving it a moment's thought. Here was a spiral staircase the greater part of which purported to be choked up with, as it were, its own detritus—and this within a massive tower which showed no sign of having been damaged in any really major way. So what was the explanation? Appleby thought he saw the answer: *a hastily improvised and very tolerably cunning construction of a large place of concealment.* Take a picturesque guess, he told himself, and complete the picture. Cromwell or such another has surrounded Treskinnick Castle and the cannon-balls are flying, are here and there bringing down little mountains of shattered masonry. Everything that ever was aboard the *Nuestra Señora del Rosario* is due to be dis-covered and carried off by these atrocious rebels. So the stuff is bundled into the topmost chamber but one in the North Tower, and the staircase immediately above it and below given a hearty bashing and jammed up with stone from the shattered battlements of the castle or wherever—and with the hope that the final effect is going to pass as the result of cannonade. It is, of course, no more than a desperate gamble. And whether the gamble paid off had been a speculation occupying the spacious mind of Ambrose Sutch.

Soberly, Sir John Appleby reconsidered these extrava-gant conjectures, and decided that they weren't entirely

147

prompted by the reading of much romantic fiction in youth. The thing just *was* feasible. Sutch had done well to investigate. And he would do well to investigate too.

He knelt down and thrust an arm through the hole. It moved freely around in vacancy. If there were a watcher in the chamber below, it would appear to him that a minatory hand had suddenly appeared as from the heavens, dramatically pointing at the hoarded treasure of the Digitts. Appleby withdrew his arm, and peered through the hole instead. Nothing except utter darkness was to be observed. No ray of light appeared to penetrate to the mysterious chamber. A torch was essential for any further discovery, and he hadn't such a thing any nearer than in his car outside the castle. Some sort of periscope would be useful as well. But such things don't lie around.

'Good-morning, sir,' a respectful voice said from somewhere behind him. 'Can I help you in any way?'

Appleby stood up and dusted himself down. He had just made an important discovery which others ought to have made before him—possibly even this constable who had now appeared in the muniment room. Nevertheless Appleby found himself feeling slightly foolish. It was quite a long time since he had pursued the art of criminal investigation to the extent of peering through a key-hole (or some such aperture) and making what he could of what was thus revealed. It would have been more becoming, he told himself, if some keen young detective officer under Craig's command had brought off this particular triumph of espionage.

'Thank you,' he said, 'but I've finished what I've been up to. Just what have you got there?' There had appeared through the window, and behind the constable, two men carrying a large metal contraption.

148

'It's a grille to put up over this window, sir. Inspector Craig doesn't want to set a guard over the place any longer. But he feels it ought to be kept under lock and key until after the inquest at least. It won't take these men above an hour to do the job, and I'm to hand one of the keys to you now, if you care to have it, sir.'

'I think not.' Appleby shook his head briskly. 'If I want to come back here I'll contact the Inspector. Is he, do you know, thinking of returning to the castle this afternoon?'

'I think not, sir.'

'Then get hold of him on the telephone as soon as you can, and ask him to come and take a look at this.' Appleby had beckoned to the constable, and was now pointing to the late Dr Sutch's effort as a stone-mason. 'Take a good look at it, Constable, so that you can describe it accurately.'

'Yes, sir.'

'And tell him that, in my opinion, it would appear to bear upon the Spanish hypothesis.'

'Upon what, sir?'

'The Spanish hypothesis.'

'The Spanish hypothesis, sir. Message understood.'

Appleby, although he doubted whether these last words were quite true, judged the lack of expression with which they had been uttered to be to the credit of this young man's training. He relaxed a little.

'And now I'll get out before they turn this place into a cage,' he said. 'I've no wish to become one more animal in that zoo.'

'You'd be better preserved than most of them, sir.'

'Thank you very much, Constable. But—by the way—always choose your man before you make your joke.'

'I did, sir.'

'Young man, I'm afraid you'll go far. Be so good, incidentally, as to tell Inspector Craig that I am driving over to Budleigh Salterton.'

'Budleigh Salterton, sir. Very good.'

'And breaking the speed limit,' Appleby added, as he climbed through the window.

Part Three

BUDLEIGH SALTERTON AND AFTER

XVII

BUT IN FACT Appleby covered the first part of his route at
a very moderate pace. He couldn't represent to himself that
he was on any sort of urgent mission. He wasn't going to
make history in Budleigh Salterton by defusing the terror-
ist's bomb or arresting the assassin's knife. An afternoon
call on an elderly lady was all that he had in mind, and
there was no hurry about that. Even if he stopped at a pub
for a late lunch he'd probably be a little early in terms of the
ordinances of Budleigh Salterton society.

Yet he had hastened away from Treskinnick Castle.
That young policeman—who could judge his man—might
even have thought him hot on the scent, and this he
couldn't honestly claim was the case. He did, indeed, now
believe that he knew how Dr Ambrose Sutch had died. The
narrow truth of that matter had come to him as he stood
contemplating that deceased scholar's surprisingly deft
performance with mallet and chisel on the floor of the
muniment room. But the why and wherefore of the affair
was still obscure to him, and he doubted whether the true
history of the *Nuestra Señora del Rosario* was going to clear it
up. It was undeniable that the ill-fated galleon had rather
notably hove up on his horizon that morning; had come
grandly in, so to speak, with all sails spread. When he had
shoved aside that (far from well-preserved) Monarch of the
Glen the revelation beneath his nose had been a revelation
authentic enough. But it was, his instinct told him, a little
off-centre from the heart of the mystery, just as that

peep-hole was a little off-centre on the floor of the muniment room. But what about Miss Deborah Digitt (to whom he had so abruptly been prompted to make his way) being positively peripheral? In point of mere physical remove that was certainly her station in the case. When, for instance, Ludlow had been aware of much mysterious coming and going, and of sundry nocturnal flickerings in the North Tower, it was scarcely to be supposed that this elderly spinster had broken into the castle and was up to mischief.

But at least Appleby had somehow received the impression that Miss Digitt had a lucid mind, and that she was interested in family history: neither of these being attributes with which it was possible to credit that family's present head. Send her out on a country—or marine—walk, and she would probably know whether she had, or had not, seen a helicopter. Incidentally, did she at this moment know anything whatever about the existence, let alone the sudden death, of Dr Sutch? It seemed likely that nobody at Treskinnick would much bother to inform this obscure relation of the distressing affair. Or would Lady Grace Digitt have done so? Lady Grace had spoken as if Miss Digitt were yet to be tackled about those problematical papers. No doubt Sutch's death-plunge had been featured in the press, but it wouldn't have been with any prominence in the newspapers Miss Digitt was likely to read. It seemed conceivable that Appleby, like some messenger in high tragedy, was going to arrive with the news of totally unapprehended disaster.

It certainly wasn't with this intention that he was climbing up to Dartmoor now. He wanted to receive information, not to disseminate it. And it was information about Adrian Digitt's remains. Here, he saw, was the explanation of his having set out so rapidly to exchange the north coast of

Cornwall for the south coast of Devon. He didn't want that galleon creeping up on him. Or not to the exclusion, as it were, of the other side of the penny. He'd started out from those confounded papers, and he'd stick to them if he could. And Miss Deborah Digitt was likely to know more about them than anybody else—or than anybody else still in the land of the living. If they were extant, they might even be legally her property. And certainly not a dozen words of Adrian's could be converted for the first time from manuscript into print without her permission being obtained. Or at least Appleby believed that to be the law. Of course judges—he thought gloomily, and on the strength of considerable acquaintance with their ways—can contrive to bring in any judgement they please upon any subject under the sun. It's their way of vindicating natural justice, often enough, against the imbecilities of what they are appointed to administer. But the results can be disconcerting at times.

He had reached that point, a little short of Two Bridges, at which one can enjoy, if one wants to, an advantageous view of Princetown Prison. Another facet of the law, Appleby told himself—and accelerated as he did so. He had never much cared for penal establishments, and in his later years had even discovered a fondness for those detected criminals who contrive to meet with fatal misadventure or to make away with themselves rather than enter such dismal receptacles. What if this respectable if decayed female at Budleigh Salterton proved to have been master-minding (or mistress-minding) highly criminal activities in the abode of her ancestors, and had to be huddled into Holloway as a result of his own good offices? It seemed, indeed, highly improbable. But a detective's life is full of nasty surprises. He wouldn't like it a bit.

Budleigh Salterton, although no doubt provided with a base and brickish skirt somewhere or other, appeared on immediate view to consist of two large hotels, a single narrow street much impeded by motor-cars of the more prosperous sort, and a scattering of villas of varying consequence straggling up a slope overlooking the sea. Among these last Miss Deborah Digitt proved to occupy what might be called a middling station, her house being less spacious but more elegant than those immediately adjoining it. There was a small garden at the front, and in it at the moment an elderly man of decent appearance was trimming a low box hedge which had the look of having been quite sufficiently attended to already. Appleby passed the time of day, and at this the elderly man straightened up and respectfully touched his cap. It was evident that, within the curtilage of Miss Digitt's domain, antique ways prevailed. Appleby rang a bell, and it was answered almost at once by an equally elderly maidservant.

'We don't give at the door,' this person said promptly.

'Is Miss Digitt at home?' Making this ritual inquiry, Appleby had charitably to assume that the eyesight of Miss Digitt's retainer must be much impaired. He had to conjecture, too, that the superior inhabitants of Budleigh Salterton were constrained to cope, surprisingly, with a surge of mendicants against their gates. The maidservant, however, had now opened the door more widely and admitted him to a small hall. She then picked up a silver tray and positioned it accurately a couple of inches in front of the visitor's chest.

'I can take up your card,' she said austerely.

Appleby produced what was thus demanded. As it was some years since he had done anything of the kind, the small oblong of pasteboard when deposited proved to be picturesquely yellowed round the edges. It occurred to him that this purblind guardian of Miss Digitt's portal might almost mistake it for a butterfly. Without more ado, however, she turned away and disappeared up a narrow staircase, her joints audibly creaking the while. Appleby looked about him. There was nothing on view except a couple of spindly chairs (not conceivably capable of supporting a human frame), some blue-and-white china, a large aquatint of Treskinnick Castle, and an ornately illuminated genealogical table.

The creaking renewed itself; the aged retainer came painfully down the stairs, turned, and as painfully mounted them again: Appleby made bold to suppose that he had been given some sign to follow her. And all being indeed now in order, he was shown into Miss Digitt's drawing-room.

Miss Digitt, having perhaps a little miscalculated the time at her disposal, was in the act of replacing a reference book on its shelf: it was to be presumed that she had been acquainting herself with the cardinal facts in the life of the stranger who had sent up his card to her.

'Sir John Appleby?' she said. 'Pray sit down. I do not recall our having met before. Am I to take it that this is a business—or shall I say professional—call that you are making on me?'

'Oh decidedly, Miss Digitt—and I must offer all the proper apologies. The more so, indeed, since the matter I come about is not of the most agreeable sort. I have driven over from Treskinnick, where I have been trying to assist—at the instance, I ought to say, of the Chief Constable—in elucidating an unfortunate occurence which you may have heard about.'

'I have heard of nothing of the kind, Sir John. I receive

little news of my relations there—apart from what my very dear kinsman, Charles Digitt, judges may afford me amusement from time to time.'

'I fear it isn't anything amusing that I myself have to report, Miss Digitt. At the same time I must hasten to say that it is unlikely to affect you in any intimate manner.' Appleby paused on this careful speech. He was finding Miss Deborah Digitt surprising in several ways. It was odd that she should have started off by according Charles Digitt that commendatory little chit. Appleby would somehow not have expected the young man to be anybody's very dear kinsman. Then again, Miss Digitt proved to be not as old as he had been imagining she'd be—although this still left her far from young. And there was some further oddity about her in this area, although it was hard to pin down. He had a dim sense of her as being perhaps in unfamiliar clothes, and of these clothes as clashing with her years, whatever they were. But odder still was something yet more indefinable. Miss Digitt's comportment and address, which were predictably on the stiff and formal side, were at variance with some state of feeling in her amounting, surely, to an inner excitement. Appleby had to remind himself that the Digitts as a family enjoyed a certain power to set one guessing.

'If you have something unamusing to report,' Miss Digitt said drily, 'I think I can undertake to be not amused. Pray continue.'

'You may at least have heard that there has been much interest at Treskinnick of late in the possibility of turning up the papers of Adrian Digitt, whom I understand to have been your great-grandfather.'

'I have certainly heard a good deal about that singularly futile project, Sir John.'

'From Mr Charles Digitt, no doubt.' Appleby was

again conscious that Miss Digitt had employed a somewhat surprising form of words.

'From Charles. Precisely.'

'And I suppose you will also be aware that Lord Ampersand lately engaged the services of an archivist to look into the matter—in the person of a certain Dr Ambrose Sutch.'

'The proposal was certainly made known to me.'

'But you may not have heard that Dr Sutch is dead?'

'Dear me, Sir John! I am a little astonished, I confess. I am aware of your standing, or late standing, in the Metropolitan Police. Is it possible that you have come all the way from Treskinnick to apprize me of this doubtless regrettable event?'

Appleby was about to say, 'You have not answered my question, madam'. But he decided against this briskly policemanlike manner of approach to the conundrum Miss Digitt presented. For one thing Miss Digitt, who was seated beside the chimney-piece of her drawing-room, had put out her left hand in the direction of an antique bell-pull depending from near the ceiling beside it. She was clearly minded to give the thing a tug and have her creaking parlour-maid show Sir John Appleby out. Sir John Appleby found the spectacle instructive—almost as instructive as the fact that Miss Digitt had appeared to betray a moment of indecision before the last question put to her.

'Not only is Dr Sutch dead,' he said. 'His death has taken place in circumstances that have engaged the curiosity of the police.'

'Need they engage mine?'

'Most assuredly, madam. There is a distinct possibility that the affair has its aspect of grave scandal, or worse. You must be anxious, I am sure, to have nothing of the sort reflect upon the credit and honour of your family.'

159

'Do I understand you to be saying that this man Sutch met with foul play? That he has been murdered, in short?'

'I cannot say that. The fatality is under close investigation now.'

'I see.' Miss Digitt paused. She in her turn might have been weighting a precise form of words addressed to her. 'And what more have you to ask?'

'I have to ask, among other things, whether you have ever heard of the *Nuestra Señora del Rosario*?'

For the first time, Miss Digitt was at a loss. For a moment, indeed, she looked completely blank. It was not perhaps an unreasonable reaction to so completely inconsequent-seeming a question. Quickly, however, she recovered herself.

'Of course I have, Sir John. There is an old family legend about that shipwreck and its sequel—but one completely forgotten, I should imagine, except by persons—and they are few—with some interest in our history.'

'Would Lord Skillet be one of those?'

'I understand Lord Skillet to be an entirely frivolous person. His only interests are likely to be disreputable.'

'Or Mr Charles Digitt?'

'I decline to discuss Mr Charles Digitt with you, Sir John.' Miss Digitt had drawn herself up stiffly. 'He happens to be the sole member of my family with whom I am on terms of intimacy. And with whom I would wish to be that.'

'As you please, Miss Digitt. Let me only say, then, that in what may be called the Spanish treasure there is at present a certain amount of interest at Treskinnick too. There is the thought that it may have been hidden in a chamber in the North Tower; and that the circumstances of Dr Sutch's death—how shall I put it?—interdigitate with that hypothesis.'

'I judge, Sir John, that you have taken to speaking in riddles. Pray make the particulars of this man's death known to me.'

This was a very reasonable request, and Appleby answered it, although confining himself to fact rather than inference. Miss Digitt heard him out.

'The state of that staircase,' she then said briefly, 'is clearly to be deprecated. Or, rather, having this unfortunate man go constantly up and down it was censurable. I can see no graver scandal than that.'

'Others, as it happens, had of late been going up and down it a good deal. Both Lord Skillet and his cousin, for example.'

'I can say nothing as to that. And need this interview continue?'

'Only for a moment longer, madam. I am interested in your declaring that the hunt for those papers at the castle was a singularly futile project. May I ask why you are in a position to express yourself so strongly?'

'Certainly you may. The entire body of my great-grandfather's papers are in my possession and are my property. They have been so since the death of my father many years ago.'

'In fact they are in this house now?' It was in a reasonably composed manner that Appleby asked this question. It would have taken a very keen observer indeed to detect that a moment of complete illumination had come to him.

'Indeed they are—although I am ashamed to say that until recently I was unaware of the fact. It is true that I have come across a few scattered papers from time to time. But my collection of family material is voluminous, and I have been deferring my full examination of them—thinking of the matter, perhaps, as an occupation for my later years.'

'An agreeable prospect, I don't doubt.' Miss Digitt's last words had again produced an effect of illumination, although this time of a minor order. 'May I take it that it has been Mr Charles Digitt who has succeeded in turning them up for you?'

'You may,' Miss Digitt said. And she rose and gave a tug at the bell-rope.

So Sir John Appleby was indeed shown out. He drove back to Treskinnick meditating, among other things, the mysteries of the female heart. What had made Miss Deborah Digitt so problematical was that she was living—uncertainly, no doubt—in a new world. She had even been wearing an engagement ring.

XVIII

Appleby arrived back at Treskinnick at an hour constraining him to close with the Ampersand Arms for another dinner and another night's lodging. This time it looked as if, so far as residents went, he was going to have the place to himself. Mr Cave, of course, had once again departed. It had been a shade unkind to terrify him with the threat of a charge of conspiracy on the strength of his abortive designs upon the Spanish treasure, even although it might be conceivably possible to secure his conviction if the police went about it with a will. A good deal of play could be made with those coils of rope and cord, and of the close contiguity to them in which the speleologist had first revealed himself. Appleby worked out this picture as he ate his dinner.

Dr Ambrose Sutch was the master criminal, and an inspired opportunist into the bargain. Having run up against Cave in an entirely fortuitous way, and discovered that he had at least vague designs upon wrecked treasure ships in general and the *Nuestra Señora del Rosario* in particular, he had promptly recruited the wretched man as his accomplice or tool. Granted that that inaccessible chamber in the North Tower held riches untold, it would be evident that getting at the loot and smuggling it out of the castle would be two men's task at least. Suppose that much more extensive work with mallet and chisel would make it possible to haul the stuff up into the muniment room, just where did one go from there? Very evidently, it could be said, to

163

that cave, or system of caves, almost immediately below. One would make one's preparations there. It would not be possible, without grave risk of detection, to carry through the castle and up the wooden staircase the large coil of stout rope essential for the operation to be put in hand. But the cord one could collect at any convenient time, carry in and up in something no bulkier than a brief-case, and subsequently employ to haul up the rope under cover of night. Providing these materials would have been Cave's job; Cave would cache them in the cave; and thus Sutch would not, so far, have made a single incriminating move. Even if his labours as a stone-mason should chance to be detected and interrupted, they could be passed off as no more than an excessive zeal exercised wholly in the interest of his employers.

That, it could be said, had been the plan, and its main actual risk would have been a simply physical one: were Sutch to begin enthusiastically lowering from that crazy little platform something in the nature, say, of a heavy sea-chest, the chest and the staircase and Sutch himself might all arrive at the bottom of the tower with an altogether unplanned impetus. But nothing of the sort—of precisely that sort—had happened. The breach in the floor of the muniment room was still no more than a peep-hole, and the treasure remained where for centuries it had been. And rope and cord, too, remained undisturbed where Cave had so neatly deposited them. On this theory, therefore, it would be necessary to believe that, at some anterior point in his preparations, Fate had intervened and been the end of Ambrose Sutch. It wasn't difficult to imagine that the whole sequence of events had terrified Cave very much.

Was there anybody else who would have reason to be terrified—anybody else whom this untoward turn of events would threaten to expose, as it were, as hazardously out on a limb? Appleby asked himself this question as he finished his meal and was about to leave the dining-room of the Ampersand Arms. He was arrested, however, by the entrance of Inspector Craig.

It was evident in an instant that Craig was pleased neither with himself nor with his subordinates, and that the situation required the exercise of a certain amount of tact. The tap-tap of Dr Sutch's mallet could almost be heard in the room.

'I'm so glad,' Appleby said easily, 'that you've found time to drop in. We're not without notes to compare. Let me fetch some brandy from the bar, and we can get down to it. And you musn't be too hard on your chaps for not nosing out that small activity on our deceased friend's part.'

'They've heard about it already,' Craig said darkly.

'One of them took the dramatic revelation quite well. What about some food, by the way?'

'No thank you. I had a bite an hour ago, Sir John.' Craig was recovering good humour. 'But the brandy I'll be grateful for.'

Appleby fetched the brandy. He went up to his room and dug out of his suitcase that solace of elderly and modestly prosperous men, a box of Havana cigars. Having thus adequately played the host, he left it to Craig to begin.

'It may be tricky,' Craig said. 'Just getting at that stuff, I mean. They may have to tackle clearing that spiral stair-case from the top. The main walls of the tower are immensely solid, as you'd imagine. But it's a question whether they can monkey with that floor without inviting trouble. They'll know in the morning.'

'And we'll know quite a lot by then, too,' Appleby said cheerfully. 'Perhaps Sutch was having his own doubts about more banging away.'

'Perhaps so. We've enlarged that hole a little, of course, and had a flashlight camera down. Odd bit of work. So I can tell you what's there—in a very general way.'

'I can tell you what isn't—in one specific particular, at least. The place isn't harbouring Adrian Digitt's remains.'

'It would be most unlikely, sir. But you mean you can be confident about it?'

'Yes, indeed. Didn't I let you know I was going to Budleigh Salterton? All those confounded papers are there, in the possession of Miss Deborah Digitt. If the woman isn't mad, that is. I didn't actually get a sight of them.'

'You mean that this relation of those people has had them all the time?'

'So she says, and so perhaps she believes. It's perfectly plausible, you know. She's the direct descendant of Adrian Digitt. But although plausible, Craig, it isn't true. I haven't the slightest doubt that those papers were in that muniment room no time ago at all.'

'Right up to the day of Sutch's death?'

'Possibly so—although I rather suspect they may have been moved elsewhere in the castle by then.'

Inspector Craig took some moments to digest this information and these conjectures. He sipped his brandy, drew on his cigar, and directed rather a sombre gaze on the former Commissioner of Metropolitan Police.

'And would you know,' he asked, 'how they got from Treskinnick Castle to Budleigh Salterton? Would it have been by parcel post?'

'Almost certainly not. They were taken there by Charles Digitt. He either handed them to her with a flourish, in which case she is a shocking old liar, or slipped them in among her own voluminous and very-little-examined family papers for subsequent delighted discovery by himself.'

'Why on earth should he do such a thing, Sir John? A jury would find it hard to believe.'

'A jury mayn't be asked to. And he had several reasons bundled together, I imagine. He wanted to cheat Sutch, who was proposing to do a quiet deal with him. He wanted to cheat his cousin, Lord Skillet, whom he detests. He wanted, you may say, to make fools of his whole family. And the papers, don't forget, may have a quite absurd market value.'

'But, if they were sold, wouldn't the proceeds come to him one day in any case? So wasn't he cheating himself, in a way, when he dumped them on this distant kinswoman in Budleigh Salterton?'

'He couldn't be sure there would be a penny left by the time he became Lord Ampersand—which, in any case, he may never do. As for the lady, I rather suspect him of having turned her head.'

'Turned her head!'

'She has what you might call a faded romantic streak to her. I'm not sure she doesn't believe herself to be engaged to him.'

'Good heavens, the man's a scoundrel! But we can get him for the theft, I suppose.'

'I rather doubt that, my dear Craig. Certain rights in many of those papers, you see, Miss Deborah Digitt undoubtedly has.'

'Copyright?'

'Precisely so. And the mere fact of their having been lying unknown in Treskinnick Castle by no means gives Lord Ampersand a clear title to their ownership as physical objects. Charles Digitt has merely discovered them and handed them on to Adrian Digitt's sole descendant—or perhaps has tactfully spared her perplexity by simply

167

slipping them in among her existing possessions of that sort. In fact, Craig, it all sounds to me much more a case for civil proceedings than for criminal ones. And in such affairs as these, at least, possession really often is nine-tenths of the law.' Appleby paused to examine the tip of his own cigar. 'But all this,' he said, 'seems to take us rather far from the death of Dr Sutch.'

'Seems to—or actually does?'

'Ah, that's very much a question. So let us forget about the papers for the moment, and turn to the treasure.'

'The Spanish hypothesis,' Craig said with a grin. 'But it looks as if it's a hypothesis no longer, and has turned into solid fact.'

'I'm delighted to hear it—if only because I've been spinning myself a bit of a yarn about it.'

'Is that so, sir? Well, a good many people in these parts do. Spin themselves a yarn, I mean, about Spanish gold. I think I've mentioned that before. And about its causing us a certain amount of trouble and annoyance from time to time. Which is why I haven't been in a hurry to believe in this Digitt hoard. Well, I've seen it now, and seeing has to be believing.'

'*Seen* it, Craig? You're ahead of me. I haven't seen the papers.'

'To say I've seen *it*, Sir John, would be to stretch a point. But I've seen what it's stowed away in. In the photographs, that is.'

'Photographs you've secured through that spy-hole, you mean?'

'Just that. What shows up isn't by any means all that may be down there. But it's enough to be going on with, you may say. There's three massive chests—iron-bound, pad-locked, and looking as safe as the Bank of England.'

'Well, well!' Appleby seemed much impressed. 'When archaeologists dig down into ancient tombs, you know, they frequently find that the wandering Bedouin or who-ever have succeeded in rifling them long ago. You are sure those chests haven't been neatly broken into at the back?'

'Of course I'm not sure of anything of the sort.' Craig was not quite pleased by this carefree conjecture. 'Perhaps Charles Digitt has been miraculously in on this loot too, and has poured it out at the feet of his beloved. We can only wait and see, sir.'

'Yes, of course. By the way, are Lord Ampersand and his family waiting and seeing too? I mean, have you told them about the discovery of this Aladdin's Cave?'

'Yes, sir. I rang up the Chief Constable, and he said it wouldn't be proper not to inform Lord Ampersand of what had happened at this stage of the investigation.'

'I suppose Brunton was right.' Appleby didn't say this with much conviction. 'Did Lord Ampersand show much interest in this prospect of sudden wealth within his grasp?'

'I doubt whether his mind got round to seeing it quite in that way, Sir John. He said he'd tell his wife, and then he said something about having to walk the dogs. Perhaps the penny would drop when he got under full steam with them.'

'Several pennies will drop here and there in the castle, I don't doubt. Is the whole family at home still?'

'I believe so.'

Appleby glanced at his watch.

'It's a pity,' he said, 'that we can't clear this thing up tonight. But I'll have a go, Craig, round about breakfast time.'

XIX

Faithful to this resolution, Appleby was back at Treskinnick Castle by nine o'clock on the following morning,
and the first person he came upon was Lord Skillet, who
was pacing up and down a small terrace which lay outside
the moat on the landward side of what a guidebook might
have called the frowning pile. Lord Skillet was frowning
too, and he sufficiently forgot the canon of *noblesse oblige* to
utter the words, 'Good God, you here again!' as Appleby
came up to him. Appleby wasn't perturbed. The meeting
was entirely agreeable to his wishes, however disagreeable
the heir of the Ampersands proposed to be.

'Good-morning,' Appleby said. 'I think we may hope for
a sunny day. And, of course, a busy day as well. For I
suppose you must have heard the remarkable news?'

'About this nonsense in the North Tower? Of course I
have. And my father has taken it into his head to get excited
about it. What he ought to be is indignant. There are half a
dozen damned impertinent fellows up there now, doing
their best to pull the place to pieces. And without so much
as a by-your-leave, curse them!'

'I hardly think that can be so, Lord Skillet. The police
would initiate or permit nothing of the kind without your
father's permission.'

'If he gave them that sort of nod, it's because he is
addle-pated enough to believe that there's money in it. He
sees these fellows handing him over a healthy young fortune in a sack. Absolute tripe! Currency immured like that

is treasure trove and will be impounded by the Crown. Which in this day and age is another word for the bloody proles. Simply go as a hand-out on the dole queues. The old dotard ought to be getting out an injunction to stop the bastards.'

'It would need a very clever counsel to argue that one successfully, I fear. A judge in chambers, you see, would have to be told about our little troubles over Dr Sutch, and he would feel that the police had better be left to the exercise of their judgement. You have to face it, Lord Skillet. The day of cosy private plans in the matter of the *Nuestra Señora del Rosario* are over.'

'What the devil do you mean by that?'

'And Dr Sutch is over too. After life's fitful fever he sleeps well. But the same can't be said of the law. The law's wide awake. And, sir, it has its eye on you.'

Lord Skillet (as was extremely reasonable) failed to care for this speech. He turned first pale and then crimson, and in his eye there was something that made Appleby wonder—not for the first time—whether in a lurking way he was not a little mad. Had a halberd, falchion, broad-sword, poignard or other mediaeval weapon been to hand he would undoubtedly have despatched this insolent knight in a feudal and arbitrary fashion. As things were, he produced a spluttering sound and took a couple of alarmed steps backwards—thereby being in some danger of tumbling into the moat.

'In fact,' Appleby said, 'there is a situation that you and I may usefully have a quiet word about. Wouldn't you agree?'

'Certainly not! I won't hear a word from you. Just what are you up to?'

Appleby judged this brief but confused speech to be

satisfactory. The tiresome Archie was undoubtedly among those at Treskinnick who were dead scared by the developing situation.

'I am suggesting, Lord Skillet, that you and I might confer—simply in a few minutes of quiet but revealing talk—about the murder of your father's unfortunate archivist.'

'You're talking nonsense. The man wasn't murdered.'

'Possibly not. I don't know that I'd care to be dogmatic at this stage. But Inspector Craig's mind undoubtedly inclines that way.'

'I tell you it's nonsense. Sutch couldn't have been murdered. There was nobody there to murder him.'

'That depends—doesn't it?—on what one means by "there". It is certainly difficult to see how there could have been anybody up there in the muniment room with him. But even that isn't impossible. The North Tower has three free-standing sides, after all. A man might slither down a rope, you know, and slip into the castle undetected. Again, there are adjacent parts of the castle which can't be said exactly to command the tower, but do attain to something over half its height. And from one or two points I find that at least a part of that platform must have been visible. So part of Dr Sutch may have been visible too—and in a highly vulnerable situation. He had only to be startled into losing his balance, you might say, and he might take a grab at something, manage only a heavy fall, and go tumbling down, staircase and all.'

'That doesn't sound like murder to me.'

'Does it not? It would depend, I believe, entirely upon what the law calls *mens rea*: intent, in plain English. By the way, when you were a boy did you ever amuse yourself with a catapult?'

172

As what might be called war-of-nerves stuff, all this nonsense on Appleby's part was yielding a satisfactory result—as appeared when Lord Skillet now abruptly changed ground.

'Anyway,' he said, 'why should anybody want to make away with the man? Are you thinking of those damned papers?'

'They are certainly not absent from my mind. But what I'd say in general is this: that Dr Sutch was a man with a flair for discovering things. But equally, perhaps, with a weakness for being discovered as having discovered them. And, conceivably, for doing, or proposing to do, deals. In such circumstances, other interested parties might become a little impatient with him. So let us by all means discuss the papers—the literary remains, to put it more grandly, of Adrian Digitt. What is your own view, Lord Skillet, of their having turned up at Budleigh Salterton?'

'Of their having *what*?' It would have been hard to believe that Lord Skillet wasn't genuinely astounded. 'What the devil are you talking about?'

'Dear me, I thought you'd have been bound to know about that by now. Miss Deborah Digitt has the whole lot and says she always has had. But without knowing it, you see. Your cousin, Charles Digitt, has quite recently turned them up for her. He's rather thick with her, it seems.'

'Just how have you got hold of this absurd story? Was it from Charles himself?'

'Definitely not. I called on Miss Digitt yesterday afternoon. We had quite a friendly chat.'

'Then damn your impertinent interference in our private family affairs!' For a moment it looked as if Lord Skillet were again meditating physical violence. Then he recovered himself. 'But if there's anything in it,' he said slowly, 'it looks as if Charles may have a good deal to answer for.'

'Ah.'

'And as if Sutch got no more than his deserts.'

'A most interesting suggestion. Would you care to elaborate on it?'

'I can't imagine what Charles could think to gain by smuggling those papers into that old woman's keeping. But, if you're telling the truth, that's what he did. And Sutch must have connived at it.'

'I rather doubt at least that last statement.'

'Very well.' Lord Skillet was obviously thinking rapidly. 'Sutch had found the papers, and had told Charles—or say Charles had simply discovered the fact. They removed them together to some temporary hiding-place in the castle, and started bargaining about a share-out. Then Charles did the spot of double-crossing you'd expect of him, made off with the stuff, and dumped it on that rascally old hag in Budleigh What-d'ye-call-it.'

'Then?'

For the first time, the resourceful Archie hesitated. A moment later, he took a plunge.

'It left Sutch,' he said calmly, 'inconveniently well-informed.'

'You have your own flair, my dear sir. Shall we call it for detective investigation? Sergeant Cuff or Inspector Bucket could scarcely do better.'

'More damned policemen around the place? I've only met somebody called Craig—and pretty thick he is.'

'You are in error about him, I fear. But we are losing sight—are we not?—of the *Nuestra Señora del Rosario*. Perhaps we ought again to address our minds to that. For here is

174

something else that Sutch knew about. And again, perhaps, he was by one means or another constrained to share his knowledge with somebody else. But this time, of course, there was no making off with the booty to another part of England. For there it is still—and with the police peering down a hole at it. But that is to run a little ahead. We are merely establishing the fact that the learned but sadly acquisitive Dr Sutch was a man considerably at risk, perhaps from more quarters than one. The more one considers the matter, the more surprised one is that he survived as long as he did.'

'I wish I'd never found the bloody man.'

'That may well be.' Appleby glanced curiously at Lord Skillet. It would have been accurate to say that he was well softened-up—indeed, scared out of his wits. And somewhere in the castle, Appleby imagined, his cousin Charles Digitt was in much the same case. The plot thickened. Or, rather, it might be said to be thinning, since it was destined soon entirely to dissipate itself. His wife hadn't been wildly out, after all, in her estimate of when the mystery of the Ampersands might resolve itself.

'Another thought occurs to me,' Appleby said. 'And perhaps I may be permitted to share it with you, since you have indulged me so far, Lord Skillet. Suppose two persons, each with their several reasons for wishing Dr Sutch not exactly too well. Might not a little sharing bob up again? They needn't be precisely friendly with one another—but then adversity can make strange bed-fellows. And two might be better than one for the purpose of coping with the situation. Would you say there might be something in that?'

'I don't intend to say anything. I've had enough of this. And it's all highly irregular.'

175

'That puts the matter mildly, does it not?'

'You know perfectly well what I mean. You have no standing here whatever. I shall speak to the Home Secretary.'

'You may be lucky, Lord Skillet, if you don't find yourself speaking to the Lord Chief Justice, or someone of that order.'

At this grim moment there came an interruption in the person of Inspector Craig. He had emerged from the castle, spotted the conference going on, and come hurrying forward.

'Good-morning, sir,' he said. 'Good-morning, my lord. They've risked it and got through, I'm glad to say. Knocked out something like a man-hole, and put in what they call a collar. No danger at all. And anybody can go down that pleases.'

XX

EVERYBODY PLEASED, SINCE it had appeared to the
mind of Lord Ampersand that a momentous family occasion was about to transact itself. As Warren Hastings had
restored the fortunes of his house from the wealth of India,
so was Lord Ampersand now to do from the wealth of what
he thought of vaguely as the Spanish Main. Before under-
taking those severer studies at Eton and Christ Church
which had distinguished his later youth he had no doubt
dipped into romances turning upon that sort of thing. And
these were informing his intelligence now.

Even Lady Ampersand and her daughters had made
that emergency ascent to the muniment room up the zigzag
of ladders—and from thence the shorter but not less tricky
climb down a further ladder through the narrow aperture
now communicating with the treasure house below. Ludlow, moreover, was in attendance. Judging that this portentous occasion might be of a protracted order, he had
brought up a basket containing china and a couple of
vacuum flasks. At an appropriate moment he would no
doubt formally announce that coffee was served.

Not that the chamber now revealed beneath the muniment room was at all a nice place for a party, and Lady
Ampersand must be said to have taken against it at once.
It was dusty and cobwebby and presumably alive with
spiders. It contrived to have a bad smell which possibly
had something to do with bats or owls. Except for a
glimmer of light that now came from above, it seemed to

177

be a region of darkness immemorial and entire. The police, indeed, had run in an electric flex to which they had connected a single powerful bulb. Unfortunately they were having trouble with this, and when Appleby arrived the place was being intermittently plunged back into repellent gloom while they tinkered. Craig was displeased, the two constables on the job were agitated, Lord Skillet plucked up spirit to make contemptuous remarks, Charles Digitt judged it amusing to strike up with that ditty in *Treasure Island* which celebrates fifteen men on a dead man's chest.

There was, of course, nowhere to sit down. There was nothing in the chamber at all except what Craig had described to Appleby as three massive chests. They were massive rather than large, and although impressively impregnable-looking and antique seemed not quite up to accommodating that amount of bullion, specie and whatever which might fairly have been expected to go sailing in the *Nuestra Señora del Rosario*. Of course what they contained was likely to be wealth in a very concentrated form indeed. But great expectations had been aroused, and the general effect was now a shade in the way of anticlimax. The company stood round staring at the chests rather in the manner of passengers thinking to identify their luggage at an airport.

'There are those big padlocks, my lord,' Inspector Craig was saying. 'But it turns out that we shall not need the services of a locksmith. They look formidable, but actually no key has been turned in them. So, barring a little rust on the bolts, and corrosion in the hinges and so forth, we ought to be able to open up without doing much damage. It's entirely as your lordship pleases.'

'Aren't there any legal formalities?' Charles Digitt asked.

'An inventory to be made by officers of a court, or something of that sort? I only put the question.'

'Thank you, Mr Digitt,' Craig said with gravity. 'But I have inquired into the point, and we are quite in order. The constables and myself, and of course Sir John, will be considered as very adequate independent witnesses to what takes place.'

'Capital!' Lord Ampersand said. 'Go ahead, my dear sir. We needn't begin actually counting the money, you know. Not at this moment. Just get a general idea of the thing, eh?' He glanced round the gathering. 'Sad,' he added unexpectedly, 'that that poor fellow Sutch ain't here. Quite a moment for him, it would have been bound to be.'

Nobody found anything to say to this. The two constables addressed themselves to prizing up the lid of the first chest. It came free with a good deal of creaking. Most inconsequently, Appleby was reminded of Miss Deborah Digitt's maid. Lord Ampersand advanced and peered inside.

'What's that on top?' he asked. 'Deuced odd thing. Little picture of quite a pretty girl. What do you make of that?'

'The Blessed Virgin, Uncle.' Charles Digitt had stepped forward too. 'But having nothing to do with our *Señora del Rosario*, I fear. Although here, for that matter, is an actual rosary as well. And—good Lord!—rather a nice wooden crucifix into the bargain. But French, I'd say, rather than Spanish.' He rummaged rapidly in the chest. 'Apart from that, nothing but books.'

'*Books?*' Lord Ampersand repeated blankly, and not exactly as a book-lover might utter the word. 'What the devil do you mean, Charles?'

'I think I know what I mean. And probably Sir John does too.' Charles laughed harshly. 'Damned good!' he said. 'Open up the other two treasure chests at once.'

This was done, and amid mounting stupefaction the contents were turned out on the dusty floor. *Books. Nothing but books.*

'Sir John,' Lady Grace Digitt said with dignity, 'you are a person, I have been told, of considerable cultivation. Pray explain all this to us if you can.'

'I don't think it's very difficult.' Appleby wasn't entirely amused at being credited with a smattering of letters. 'What we have here is quite a large accumulation of works of Catholic devotion. And a good deal of polemical theology, no doubt. The collection may be of some interest to scholars. Here is Polanco's *Vita Ignatii Loiolae*. And the *Acta quaedam* too. This, in fact, was the treasure that certain past Ampersands thought cunningly to hide away when Cromwell's soldiers were surrounding them.' Appleby looked up soberly. 'These books must have been very dear to somebody.'

This edifying conclusion to the hunt for Spanish gold unfortunately failed to please Lord Ampersand. Lord Ampersand, in fact, promptly treated himself to some species of mild fit, and there was confusion as a result. Ludlow hastened forward with coffee. And then suddenly, and to a freezing effect, the hollow chamber resounded to a maniacal laugh. Appleby turned round in time to see the bottom of the ladder disappearing through the hole in the roof. A moment later there was a tremendous crash; the fraudulent treasure house shook on its foundations; the single glaring light went out. Lord Skillet had withdrawn from the scene, and in doing so had contrived to topple a massive flagstone on the only exit from it. A series of further muffled clatters told that he was successively dislodging the ladders by which he was now descending to *terra firma*. The baffled treasure-seekers were immured within the arena of their fiasco.

One of the constables had a torch. It gave a pretty poor light, but one good enough to show that Lord Ampersand had recovered. Lady Ampersand encouraged him to let Ludlow pour him more coffee. Lady Ampersand appeared not particularly discomposed.

'It has really been quite some time,' she said to Appleby in the gloom, 'since Archie had one of these little episodes. They run in the family, it seems. My husband's family, that is—not mine. I suppose he was disappointed at our finding nothing but all those books.'

'As Sutch would have been too,' Charles Digitt said. 'And what will Archie be doing now? Chewing the drawing-room carpet, or climbing up the curtains?'

'Oh, nothing so uncomfortable as that.' Lady Ampersand spoke reassuringly, as if anxious to set her nephew's mind at ease in the matter. 'He just makes off for a time, and perhaps plays one of his rather silly jokes. And then he comes home and tells us about it. I wonder whether we shall get back to the castle in time for luncheon. I believe there are to be lamb chops. Ludlow, are there to be lamb chops for luncheon?'

'I believe so, my lady.'

'That will be very nice. And meanwhile we must resign ourselves, must we not? But I shall be disappointed if I have to miss my Noah's Ark. Inspector Craig, am I likely to do that?'

'I don't know, madam.' Craig was perplexed and irritated. 'We are in something uncommonly like a Noah's Ark ourselves. But it can only be a matter of minutes, I imagine, before somebody tumbles to the fact. It's getting up the ladders again that will take time.'

'Anything up to an hour, I expect,' Appleby said. 'Might it be a good opportunity to explain to you just what happened to Dr Sutch?'

'This is rather a gloomy setting,' Charles Digitt said, 'to be told about a murder.'

'No doubt. But there was, as it happens, no murder. Dr Sutch's death was an accident.' Appleby paused on this. 'But an accident, I must admit, of rather a peculiar kind.'

XXI

IN THE LOW light from the single electric torch the two
constables might have been observed to glance at one
another apprehensively. If this high-ranking person was
about to pronounce upon confidential matters they would
in normal circumstances be expected to make themselves
scarce. But circumstances were far from normal, since the
entire company was virtually shut up in a box. But Inspector Craig, as Appleby would have expected of him, took
charge of this aspect of the matter.

'Excellent,' Craig said. 'I'm sure Lord Ampersand and
his family, just as much as myself and my own officers,
would like to see this confused affair cleared up in double-
quick time. But I wonder whether we can find Lady
Ampersand a seat? Richards, see what you can do with
some of the larger of those books.'

At this Constable Richards (who probably had a nasty
feeling that he ought to have been watching Lord Skillet
like a lynx throughout the past half-hour) sprang gratefully
into activity. As a result, Lady Ampersand was presently
accommodated on a sort of bench constructed out of substantial quartos and folios. On this she seated herself with
composure, rather in the manner of Dame Theology as
conceived by some mediaeval mind. It seemed likely that
there were those present who would have preferred to see
her in the character of *Usuria*, plumped down on Spanish
money-bags.

'It must be understood,' Appleby began, 'that what I

183

have to say is bound at times to reflect disadvantageously upon the conduct and motives of certain of the persons concerned. That must be put up with, I'm afraid.'

'Are you talking about my son?' This, which came from Lord Ampersand with a sharpness doing surprising credit to his intellectual grasp of the situation, didn't find Appleby in any doubt.

'Lord Skillet,' he said, 'has certainly behaved in an odd and reprehensible manner. He has done so this morning, as I think you must agree. Just what he is up to now, I can't say. Probably something freakish rather than vastly criminal. He appears subject—as indeed his mother has told us—to a good deal of mental aberration from time to time. But let me begin.

'From the first there have been what we may term two magnets in this affair. The first has been represented by the notion that hidden somewhere in Treskinnick Castle there has been this hoarded and concealed treasure of Spanish origin. There is a family legend to that effect, and it connects with what I take to be an actual historical occurrence which other people have known about as well: the shipwreck in the early seventeenth century of a vessel called the *Nuestra Señora del Rosario*. But, if that is fact, the legend is moonshine. What was veritably tucked away here at the time of the siege, we have just discovered.'

'*Books*,' Lord Ampersand said darkly—and then a new thought seemed to strike him. 'Uncommonly *old* books. Might be worth a lot of money, eh? Astonishing, I'm told, what people will now pay for rubbish.'

'No doubt the collection may have some moderate pecuniary value.' Appleby took up this hopeful suggestion patiently. 'But it would be unwise to repose much confidence in it. These are probably very run-of-the-mill

184

theological works, together with a great many manuals of homiletic character, designed in the main, it may be, to assist female devotion. They are not likely to have any large appeal today. But let me continue.

'The second magnet, of course, has been Adrian Digitt's papers. These do exist, and have been discovered. They have been lately within the control of Mr Charles Digitt—have they not, Mr Digitt?—and he, having judged them to be the rightful property of Miss Deborah Digitt of Budleigh Salterton, has in fact returned them into the possession of that lady. They are with her now.'

There was a short silence. How Charles Digitt took the making of this communication to his kinsfolk, it was too dark to see. The Ampersands and their daughters were presumably stupefied by such a revelation of treachery in their midst.

'So much is now clear,' Appleby continued. 'I now come to Dr Ambrose Sutch. He is to be described as an acute, ingenious, and—I fear—singularly unscrupulous man. He was introduced into the castle by Lord Skillet—not, I imagine, without the thought of being exploited to Lord Skillet's private advantage were he actually to discover the papers. He did discover them. But he also discovered something else. The fabled Spanish treasure was very much in his mind, and it was, I believe, a chance remark of Mr Digitt's that put him on what he supposed to be the track of them. To an architect there would appear to be something fishy—it is probably the right term—about the manner in which the spiral staircase admitting to the upper ranges of this tower had been rendered impassable. Dr Sutch investigated. He investigated with the aid of a mallet and chisel. They are implements, as it happens, that we have not heard the last of.

185

'Take the papers first. Sutch's discovery of them became known to Mr Digitt, who had been much about the place, and Sutch was constrained to agree to removing them elsewhere in the castle while the two men bargained over them.'

'Bargained over them!' Lord Ampersand exclaimed.

'Just that. Shall we put it, for the moment, that Mr Digitt was so righteously convinced of Miss Deborah Digitt's being entitled to them that he entered upon a course of conspiracy with Dr Sutch—whom he was determined, to put it bluntly, to double-cross. Dr Sutch was much too clever not to be aware of this. So Mr Digitt and Sutch became, in a sense, adversaries. There was this booty—if the word be not too coarse—to quarrel over.

'But now I pass again to the supposed treasure. Here it was Lord Skillet who did a little successful spying: he too, as you are aware, was much about the place.

'You will see that it would be much to the advantage of Lord Skillet and Mr Digitt severally were Sutch at this point to disappear from the scene. But, equally, it would be to *his* advantage if *they* did—or if even one of them did. It was a dangerous state of affairs.'

At this point in Appleby's exposition Inspector Craig might have been distinguished as moving over to his subordinates and murmuring to them in an instructive manner. They had let Lord Skillet slip. If Charles Digitt gave trouble—suddenly producing, it might be, a lethal weapon—they were to pounce.

'I may say that Dr Sutch, a resourceful man, now himself brought into the picture a more or less reliable confederate of his own: a person called Cave, who was to assist him in smuggling away the treasure when he succeeded in getting down to it. The plan involved, in a manner I need not at the moment detail, a length of rope and a length of cord. These, Sutch caused Cave to deposit in a cavern which, as it happens, lies far below this chamber in which we are at present so ludicrously incarcerated.

'But now Sutch had a brilliant idea: nothing less than the employment of that rope and cord for a quite new purpose. At an appropriate time he would loop the rope round the platform of that insecure and rotting wooden staircase. He would then descend to the shore, having achieved a perfectly constructed booby-trap. If he caught Lord Skillet on one of his visits to the muniment room, he could himself become the undisputed possessor of the treasure; if he caught Mr Digitt, he would be in a similar position in regard to the papers. He was in the happy position of profiting handsomely whether he achieved one murder or another.

'Unfortunately for Sutch, his flair for improvisation carried him a little further—or so it is reasonable to conjecture. While working industriously at the enlarging of his spyhole, I imagine, it occurred to him that mallet and chisel might be put to a further use. He had doubts about that powerful tug from below. He decided—and it was a courageous decision in its way—to go out to the platform and do a little tinker with the masonry of the tower at one or two accessible points at which the supports of the staircase were embedded in it. He succeeded in this, and returned happily to his operation in the interior. But he had been a little too radical in the matter, and when he next stepped—cautiously, no doubt—out on the platform down it went without any assistance of a tug from below, and this very evil man with it. The enginer, as Hamlet has it, had been hoist with his own petard.'

187

XXII

IT HAD BEEN in various ways an uncomfortable morning—and not the less because there had been several hitches in freeing the prisoners of the tower. Lady Ampersand, with her jigsaw hour in jeopardy, more than once remarked that it had been too bad of Archie. Inspector Craig consulted Appleby on the propriety of placing Charles Digitt formally under arrest. Appleby was unsympathetic.

'My dear chap,' he said easily, '—whatever for? Because somebody has tried to murder him?'

'The man has impudently stolen those valuable papers . . .'

'Perhaps so. But you'd get nowhere with it in court. There's nothing but an obscure family dispute about the ownership of Adrian Digitt's remains, which are now in the possession of his sole legitimate descendant. There wouldn't be the ghost of a case, criminally regarded. Of course they can all go to law with one another, if they want to.'

'Do you know what I heard him insolently tell his uncle a few minutes ago?' Craig had drawn Appleby cautiously into a corner of the disgraced treasure chamber. 'That the papers are of enormous importance in their particular line. That there's a play almost entirely by one chap, and a lot of unknown poems by another, and a voluminous diary . . .'

'There may be a shade of exaggeration about all that, don't you think? As there has been about the treasure.'

'And then he actually told his uncle that he is going to marry the lady. It's entirely outrageous.'

'I don't see that a proposed marriage need be an outrage. Or not from a policeman's point of view.'

'And Lord Skillet is worse. Plotting blatantly to defraud . . .'

'Perfectly true, Craig. But we'd get nowhere there, either. The Ampersands wouldn't support us for a moment. The sole real villain of the piece has escaped us. He's dead.'

'And the man Cave.'

'Bother the man Cave. Ah! I think I hear them with the ladders now.'

There is always something a little ignominious about being let out of the lock-up. And this particular liberation had taken nearly three hours to achieve. The Chief Constable himself had hastened to the scene, but it turned out to be with the object of insisting that every operation involved should be carried out with a minimum of risk. There must, if it could possibly be avoided, be no scandal at Treskinnick Castle. And if through injudicious haste some workman or constable was hurried or flurried into breaking his neck, scandal there would inevitably be. In addition to which the humorously disposed Brunton was rather tickled by the thought of his old colleague John Appleby (who had outpaced him in the end) furiously raging in his narrow den.

But eventually everybody got up and then down. The Chief Constable, having uttered courteous and consolatory words to Lady Ampersand, departed again, taking Craig and his constables tactfully with him. And the lamb chops were belatedly served.

They were served to Appleby among others, since he

had seen no way of decently declining Lady Ampersand's eminently proper invitation that he should join in the family meal. The family—perhaps with some strangeness —included Charles Digitt, and Appleby supposed that the Ampersands might calculate that the presence of a stranger at the board might restrain any extreme exhibition of such passions as the late events in connection with Adrian Digitt's remains might well be expected to arouse.

As it was, it proved a chilly meal. Yet the only person to appear really angry was Ludlow, who clearly regarded his late immurement as an intolerable affront to the dignity of his position in the household. No man on earth better commands the technique of indicating a just disgruntlement than an experienced upper servant, and Ludlow laid it on thick. His manner in merely replenishing his employer's glass was so infinitely menacing that Lord Ampersand positively quailed before it. And then, towards the end of the muted banquet, and after whispered consultation with the parlourmaid, Ludlow abruptly left the room.

He returned some ten minutes later, came to a halt several feet away from the table, and spoke in a loud and formal voice.

'A telephone message from Lord Skillet, my lord. He desired me not to bring you to the instrument. I was instructed merely to give you a message.'

'A message, Ludlow?' Lord Ampersand was unashamedly nervous. 'What sort of message?'

'To the effect, my lord, that he has them.'

'Has them! Has what?'

'The call came through from Budleigh Salterton, my lord. And his lordship employed the word "retrieved". I understood him, my lord, to be referring to the family papers of which there has been some question of late. His lordship is returning to the castle with them now.'

'The bloody swine!' Charles Digitt had sprung to his feet, white and trembling. 'Deborah would never . . .'

'Charles, sit down at once.' Suddenly, Lord Ampersand was in command of his household. 'Ludlow, you may leave the room—take that goggling girl with you.' He waited for a moment, and then turned to Appleby. 'Sir John, have you anything to say about this? Is it legal, and all that?'

'Unless Lord Skillet has positively assaulted Miss Digitt, I'd say probably yes. He may have terrorized her, but she is unlikely to want to say so. And, in any case, it would be hard to prove. I am merely in the presence, I fear, of another unseemly family row.'

'Charles, dear,' Lady Ampersand said pacifically, 'Archie would naturally not want you to get away with what has certainly been a very irregular proceeding. And Cousin Deborah has not behaved well. I am quite sure that my sister Agatha would be of that opinion. As for those horrid papers, I never want to see them. I don't even want to hear of them again. They have been nothing but a vexation to us. Such nonsense about Shelley and Lord Byron and a man ridiculously called Peacock! But if the papers must come back I suppose we must put up with them. I only hope that Archie will not drive back too dangerously. He has had rather an exciting day.'

But Lady Ampersand's hope was not fulfilled. It was an hour later, when the company, after dispersing in some confusion, had for some reason reassembled in the library, that Ludlow again presented himself.

'My lord,' Ludlow said in a subdued voice, 'there has been another telephone message. A disturbing one, I am sorry to say. Lord Skillet will return to Treskinnick later in the afternoon. But not in his car, my lord.'

'What the devil do you mean, Ludlow? How can my son get back except in his car?'

'In an ambulance, my lord. The injuries are not severe, but it is thought judicious that he should travel in that manner. It has been a matter of a collision with a commercial vehicle.'

'Good God! Has anybody . . .?'

'It seems not. A tanker, my lord—the driver of which knew just how to escape when it overturned. Training, no doubt. But Lord Skillet was not quite so lucky. It appears, however, that his burns are comparatively slight. Although it is feared, indeed, that there may be some degree of permanent disfigurement. The tanker was carrying some highly inflammable chemical. His lordship's car, and everything it contained, have been totally consumed.'

There was a moment's silence, and it was Appleby who first spoke.

'So much,' Appleby said soberly, 'for the remains of Adrian Digitt.'